WOLF WARRIOR

PROJECT BLOODBORN
BOOK FOUR

CRAIG ZERF

Anglo-American Press

Wolf Warrior © 2018 by Craig Zerf

ALL RIGHTS RESERVED. This book contains material protected under International and Federal Copyright Laws and Treaties. Any unauthorized reprint or use of this material is prohibited. No part of this book may be reproduced or transmitted in Cany form or by any means, electronic or mechanical, including photocopying, recording, or by any information storage and retrieval system without express written permission from the author / publisher.

As always – to my wife, Polly and my son, Axel. You chase the shadows from my soul.

*Who's afraid of the big bad wolf
The big bad wolf, the big bad wolf
Who's afraid of the big bad wolf
Tra la la la la ...*

CHAPTER 1

Brenner was in Montana, a few miles from the Canadian border. He had contacted Griff two weeks before, telling him he needed some time alone. Then he had left San Antonio and taken a random and varied route through Arkansas, Missouri, Iowa, and South Dakota. Taking it easy. Riding slow and stopping often to eat and rest.

Healing.

He had suffered through the full moon in Missouri.

The 'Show Me' state.

Show me a werewolf.

Physically, Brenner had fully healed. Mentally ... not so much.

When he had been travelling through the backroads of Iowa he had stopped for a rest and spotted a herd of Whitetail deer. Fifteen in all. Three bucks, eight does. And four fawns, small and dappled and still unsteady on their tiny hooves.

As he had seen them he had been instantly overcome with an all-consuming killing rage and had exploded into full wolf mode. Mere minutes later he had reverted back to his human form, covered in blood, and surrounded by the ragged and dismembered remains of the herd. Even the fawns. Torn to shreds in a frenzy of killing. Killing for no reason other than a black and unstoppable rage.

A few days later, riding on a trail through South Dakota, he had come across a river barring his way. A small tributary that flowed into the larger Missouri. There were remnants of a wooden bridge, four posts and a scattering of planks. Rather than search for another place to cross he had decided to simply ford across instead.

The plan was simple, morph into Wolfman mode, carry the Harley across to the other side, continue journey.

But the moment Brenner had become the Wolfman, the world changed. A tsunami of rage crashed over him. Engulfing him in a dark sea of hatred and fury. His vision went red and the urge to kill eliminated every other emotion.

His senses went into hyperdrive. Sight,

hearing, smell. He could sense people. Far away. Perhaps ten miles or so. Their lifelight a beacon to his newfound rage. And the wolf inside him howled and roared for their demise. *They Are Weak*, it screamed.

Kill Them.

Destroy Them All.

But the tiny part of him that was still Brenner fought back. Refusing to kill for no reason. Denying the monster inside.

And with the greatest of willpower, he changed back into human form.

Then he simply lay on the ground, exhausted. His breath coming in heaving gasps. His head pounding, his muscles shuddering and twitching from the surfeit of adrenaline that had pumped through him.

'The serum,' he said to himself. It had cured his wounds, but it was not designed for him. It was tailor made for Solomon and his particular genetic makeup. With Brenner it had ramped his aggression up to unmanageable levels.

If he changed, he would kill. And he would continue to kill, until someone or something stopped him. And worse, Brenner knew the serum was not a run of the mill drug. It was not something that would simply wear off, given time. No. It was a genomic modifier. It had affected Brenner at a DNA level.

And its effects would be permanent.

His healing, speed, and strength would remain, but Ded Brenner knew one thing for certain … he could no longer risk changing into either his Wolf or his Wolfman form ever again. The risk of massive collateral damage would be far too great.

His curse was now truly a curse in both name and nature.

He was a ravening wolf trapped inside a man's body.

A beast.

And he could never be let free.

So, with a heavy heart, he rode on, heading for Montana and the Canadian border. Heading for the wilderness.

To be alone.

Or as close to alone as possible in the modern world.

CHAPTER 2

The colonel seldom left his rooms anymore. An office, bedroom, bathroom, and a small gymnasium. In fact, he had seldom left the compound in which Project Bloodborn was situated for over twenty years. A virtual hermit. An obsessive recluse bent on achieving his goal above all else.

The creation of a controllable super-soldier that would raise America's combat capabilities to a level never achievable by the enemy.

And by the enemy, the colonel meant, everybody else on the planet who was not American.

Apart from Sergeant Ded Brenner, the Project had not achieved his goal.

They had come close on many occasions. Subjects like Sergeant Solomon Hopewell, flawed by his inability to operate in the sunlight, and his absolute reliance on tri-daily doses of the serum.

Or PFC Lenny Kozlowski. As strong as a main battle tank but with a child's IQ and perception, and a tumor the size of a grapefruit in his skull.

Or countless other almost-rans. All falling at the final hurdle due to some fault or other. Cancers, faulty genetics, random diseases, or catastrophic spontaneous genetic unravelling.

Not like Brenner. Self-contained. Deadly. Operating completely autonomously and utterly unstoppable. If they could reproduce the Wolfman in a slightly more compliant host then they would have the ultimate soldier.

The ultimate weapon of mass destruction.

Then the world would know what it was to be American. Because with a thousand like Brenner, the red, white, and blue would fly proudly over the soil of every nation on earth.

All would sing the same national anthem.

Proudly American.

And now, for the first time, it looked as though the laboratory had come up with a viable alternative.

The doctor stood opposite the colonel, his laptop on the desk, a slight smile on his face. His excitement palpable.

'You say that the subjects are stable?' asked the colonel.

Doctor Mengele nodded his affirmation. Close cropped iron gray hair, dark eyes crowned by black, bushy eyebrows. Slightly misaligned teeth and a non-existent top lip.

He looked to be a fit man in his late fifties, perhaps early sixties. He was actually one hundred and six years old, exceeding the colonel's age by two whole years. A definite perk of working for The Project and its rafts of genomic and genetic research. Although they had not yet stumbled across the fountain of youth, as such, they had most definitely discovered the fountain of eternal middle-age.

'How many survived the seasoning?' continued the colonel.

At this question, Doctor Mengele's smile dropped. 'You must understand, Colonel,' he prevaricated. 'The process of adaption is an extremely rigorous one, after all, we are changing human beings into an entirely different genus. From

Homo Sapiens to an amorphous blend of *Homo* and *Hyaenidae.* We have called it, *Hyaenidae Sapiens.*'

'How many?' repeated the colonel.

'Well, of the initial sixty-four, umm … volunteers, seven have survived. Of those, three have achieved the ability to shape shift at will, although they are unstable and sometimes shift without meaning to. Sometimes to half-human mode, and other times to full beast mode. The other four are more of a permanent hybrid, the *Hyaenidae* having dominated the *Homo Sapiens* side on a permanent basis.'

'Explain,' commanded the colonel.

Mengele leaned forward and tapped his laptop, bringing the screen to life. Then he turned it to face the colonel. 'Here, it is easier to show than to tell.'

A handheld camera. The sound hollow, full of white noise. A row of cages. Each one separated from the next by three feet of empty space. The bars at least two inches thick. The doors locked with three solid steel bars and padlocked hinges. Impenetrable.

Stark electric bulbs hung from the ceiling. Concrete floor. In each cell a single steel bed with a blanket and a thin cotton mattress. Chemical toilet. A large bowl of drinking water. The cells are clearly marked from one to seven.

'Cell number one contains the Alpha,' explained Mengele. 'The strongest, and the one who is in most control of his metamorphic capabilities. We have called him Anubis. The other two shapeshifters are Osiris and Set. The four permanent hybrids are simply referred to as H-one, H-two, H-three and H-four.'

The colonel studied the screen. Cell one contained a predominantly humanoid subject. Six feet, maybe two hundred pounds. He was naked, and his musculature stood out to the point it looked somehow false. Like someone had created a rough facsimile of the human body using raw concrete. Slabs and hunks of striated muscle with little grace or form.

'Why is he standing like that?' asked the colonel. 'All hunched over. Does he have a hunchback?'

'Strictly speaking, no,' answered doctor Mengele. 'A hunched back, or Kyphosis, is an abnormality of the spine. What you are seeing is muscular. You see, one of the reasons we chose the Hyena as the primary donor is its bite is amongst the most powerful in the world. Stronger than either a lion or even a grizzly bear. And one of the main reasons for this is the huge band of muscle running from the top of the head, down the back. These are, ostensibly, the creatures jaw muscles. We retained that as one of its primary weapons. Hence, the hump of muscle.'

The colonel nodded. Not a problem. They haven't been bred for looks. As long as they can pass for human, I'm satisfied. How long until we can field test them?'

'A week,' answered the doctor. 'Maybe two. A couple of small problems with discipline we need to iron out, then we'll be good to go.'

'Well that is excellent news,' said the colonel. 'That is excellent news indeed.'

CHAPTER 3

The sign read, 'Backlash'. Underneath. Pop. 584 and an arrow pointing left.

Brenner turned off the blacktop and followed the sign, slowing down as he hit the dirt road. Twenty minutes later he was in Backlash.

He had been to a hundred similar towns before.

The dirt road had morphed back into blacktop. Albeit a rough and potholed version. The main road was wide enough for two lanes but there were no markings. Instead, patches of engine oil scattered the surface like bruises on an abused wife.

A white-clapboard, two-story courthouse and sheriff's office dominated the entrance to the town. The Stars and Stripes flew outside. As did the state flag. Blue with a gold Montana embroidered across the top. In the middle a plough, a shovel, and a pick.

Under that flew another flag. A black

and white POW-MIA flag, honoring prisoners of war and soldiers never found. Brenner raised his eyebrow in surprise. Although it wasn't exactly a contentious issue, it was unusual to see the black and white flag flying on a government building.

Outside the sheriff's office, a single white Crown Victoria. Old but well maintained, its paintwork shining like new.

The rest of the main street was the usual mixture of general store, dress shop, an outdoor supplies and gun shop, and a large diner. Perhaps twelve shops, all in all, but four of them were boarded up. A few cars parallel parked. At least three residents on horseback and a single horse drawn cart.

At the end of the street, a church. Its spire reaching high into the frigid blue sky, the front doors slightly ajar. It was a massive structure that seemed totally incongruous compared to the rest of the town. Brenner estimated it would easily fit three to four hundred people. The entire population of Backlash.

He pulled up outside the diner. A log-built structure, sturdy and squat. A plate glass window in the front, all steamed up, so it was impossible to see inside. Outside, on the door, an amateur looking sign that read, Busby's, and an artist's rendition of what Brenner assumed was a steak and mash, but actually looked more like a block of wood next to a pile of snow.

He pushed the door open. A bell tinkled as he let it close behind him. The place was large. Maybe thirty covers. Partly-exposed cooking area. A jukebox. On the right-hand side, a dance floor, a small stage, and a bar with a range of liquor behind it.

Busby's was obviously the center of the town's entertainment.

A middle-aged woman in the cooking area, pointed at a table and mouthed the words, 'Sit.'

Brenner did so.

In a short while she came over, a notebook in her hand. She wore a standard waitress outfit. Candy stripe dress, fractionally too short for both her age and her figure. A white apron, hair pulled back into a high ponytail. She had applied her makeup in a liberal fashion, eschewing subtlety in favor of concealment.

'We ain't serving breakfast,' she

informed Brenner. 'Chef stops making it at eleven.'

'Not a problem,' answered the big man as he wondered why she thought he would want breakfast in the late afternoon. 'I'm hungry, what do you recommend?'

'Chicken fried steak. Comes with mash, gravy, green beans, and corn on the cob.'

Brenner nodded. 'And a pot of coffee, thank you.'

She didn't bother to write his order down and disappeared into the kitchen without a backward glance. Moments later she returned with a Bunn flask of coffee and a mug. She didn't offer milk or sugar and Brenner didn't ask.

She poured. Brenner took a sip. The coffee was good. Really good. Fresh brewed, hot and strong, without being bitter.

'It's good.'

She smiled. 'Yep. Best in Montana. Food will be fifteen minutes or so.' With a flick of her hips she left again, leaving a faint smell of talc, cheap soap, and sweat. No perfume. Not strong enough for anyone else to smell, but easy for Brenner's heighted senses to pick up. It wasn't an unpleasant smell. It was honest. Real.

Before he was halfway through his coffee, she returned and placed the plate and cutlery in front of him. Brenner nodded his thanks and gave her a grin before he set to, eating fast and methodically. Cleaning his plate in under four minutes.

The waitress collected his cutlery and laid a plate of pie down. Apple. With a slab of cheese.

'I didn't order this,' said Brenner.

'Everyone has the pie,' the waitress informed the big man. 'It's the best in Montana.'

Brenner laughed and scooped up a mouthful. It was altogether possible she was correct. It was the best apple pie he had ever tasted. And he had tasted a few. As he was finishing the plate someone pulled up the chair on the opposite side of the table and sat.

Brenner glanced up to see an older man. Gray, short-cropped hair, large white mustache, ice-blue eyes with bushy white eyebrows and a large, straight nose that dominated his face like a lone tombstone in a field.

He also wore a sheriff's uniform.

Laying his hat on the table, he gestured to the waitress. 'Debra,' he called. 'Coffee please, sweetheart.' Then he turned to Brenner. 'Mind if I sit here a while?'

The big man felt his stomach drop. 'I got a choice?'

The sheriff grinned. 'Sure. Just say no. But then I might wonder what you got to hide.'

'Then stay,' said Brenner. 'I got nothing to hide. And look, Sheriff,' he continued. 'I'm just getting a bite to eat. Going from one place to another place. I ain't looking for trouble.'

The sheriff looked genuinely surprised. 'Well of course not,' he replied. 'Why would you be? Trouble is overrated. No, I'm simply here to have some coffee and shoot the breeze a little. Saw a new face in town and thought I'd say hello. Nothing more, nothing less. So, where you from, stranger?'

'South.'

'And where you heading?'

Brenner hesitated. 'Not sure, Sheriff,' he admitted. 'I ain't no vagrant, but, to be honest with you, I am a drifter at the moment. No fixed destination. Simply moving.'

Debra put a cup of coffee down in front of the sheriff and he nodded his thanks. 'Well, if you're looking for work, you won't have much luck here. We got the two sawmills, a few trappers, some panners, and prospectors. But on the whole the town is pretty depressed, financially speaking.' He took a sip of coffee. 'Damn, but this is good coffee,' he muttered.

'Best in Montana,' quipped Brenner.

The sheriff smiled. 'You got that right.'

Neither man spoke for a while. The sheriff studied Brenner openly, appraising him with a keen but unaggressive eye. Eventually he leaned forward. 'Where did you serve?'

'How did you know?' asked Brenner, avoiding a direct answer.

'Seen the look before. See it in the mirror every morning. Too much death. Too much killing. It leaves a mark.'

Brenner nodded. 'Where did you serve?' he returned the question.

'Vietnam.'

'If you don't mind me asking,' continued Brenner. 'Aren't you getting a little long in the tooth to be the sheriff. I mean, isn't there some kind of retirement age? After all, you've done your time.'

The sheriff chuckled. 'I don't mind you asking,' he said. 'Officially, its mandatory retirement at sixty-five. But as I'm an elected official that sorta falls by the wayside. I took this job some thirty years back and every five years the town board begged me to run again. Then a couple of years ago, there was no need to run against anyone anymore. Seemed no one else wanted the job. I got no deputies and damn near no budget. But I am the law and I suppose a town has gotta have the law, regardless of how small it is.'

'Suppose so,' agreed Brenner.

'Can I give you some advice?' asked the sheriff.

Brenner nodded.

'You can't run from yourself. I know, I tried. After 'Nam I tried to run away from the memories, the smells, the sounds. But they just stayed with me. No matter how far or how fast I ran. Finally, I stopped. Learned to accept what I was. It wasn't easy but, after a while, I got it right. You gotta stop running, my friend. And I tell you something else, if you decide to stop, then this is as good a place as any. The air is clean, the people are good, simple folk, and nobody would dream of prying unless you invited them to.'

Brenner didn't answer.

'How you set for funds?' continued the sheriff.

'I got enough to get by for a while,' answered Brenner. 'Long as I don't live the high life.'

'Tell you what. About a mile down the road there lives an old lady. Grandma Becket. She's by herself on an old homestead. With the winter coming I'm sure she'd be more than willing to give you a room in exchange for work around the place. You know, chopping wood, mending stuff. What you say? Stop running for a while and see what happens.'

Brenner nodded. 'That's mighty kind of you, Sheriff. Mighty kind. Fact, it's the first time a lawman has done me a solid for a while. I think I'll take you up on that offer.'

The sheriff stood and held his hand out. Brenner stood and took it. Shook briefly.

'Like I said. A mile down the road,'

reiterated the sheriff. 'First turning left. Can't miss the place. Tell Grandma Becket that Sheriff Colson sent you. And watch out for her. She can be a cantankerous old biddy.'

CHAPTER 4

Grandma Becket's place was a sprawling log cabin at the end of a rough graded track in the middle of thick forest. Brenner cut the engine and kicked down the stand as he dismounted.

Then he leapt sideways, rolling as he hit the ground and disappearing behind a large Douglas fir. Slowly he peeked around the trunk.

Standing in the driveway, an ancient double-barreled hammer gun in her hands, stood a diminutive old lady. The sound of her cocking the hammers had been what caused Brenner to react.

'Hoowee,' she said. 'I ain't seen a human move so fast since … well, since never. Show yourself or I'm just gonna lay down some buckshot and see what happens.'

Brenner raised his hands slowly above his head and stood. 'Afternoon, Missus Becket,' he greeted.

'It's Miss,' she replied. 'Do I know you? Come on over here so I can get a good look. Eyesight ain't what it used to be.'

He walked over and stood in front of the old lady, hands still raised at shoulder height.

She stood almost two feet shorter than him. At one stage she was probably a good five feet, but age and its corresponding erosion had shrunk her down to slightly over four and a half feet. The skin on her face was as lined as an ordnance survey map, her lips thin, hair white, and hands that hosted a party of liver spots.

But her eyes were bright green and sparkled with a life force as powerful as any Brenner had seen before.

She stared up at him, her gaze cool and appraising. Then she smiled. A symphony of wrinkles that displayed a set of white and even teeth.

'Boy, you sure are a big one,' she chuckled. 'So, what you doing on my property uninvited?'

'Sheriff Colson said to give you a call. Said you might be willing to trade a room for work. I'm looking for a place to stay for a while and I'm willing to do any odd jobs you need doing in return. Umm ... you mind pointing that shotgun the other way?'

'It's not loaded,' laughed Miss Becket. 'Look.' She pulled the trigger.

The loud boom of both barrels discharging at once shattered the still afternoon air. Twin gouts of flame spat from the barrels and the recoil lifted the tiny old lady off her feet and deposited her on her rear, some three feet away.

Once again, Brenner had to call on his superhuman speed as he swiveled out of the path of the twin cones of backshot that were aimed directly at him. A couple of balls pecked at his jacket, but he was otherwise unharmed. Still moving at superspeed he knelt beside Miss Becket.

'Are you OK, ma'am?'

'Son of a bitch,' she cried out. 'I shot you.'

'No, ma'am,' contradicted Brenner. 'You missed.'

'But how? That's impossible.'

Brenner shrugged then helped the old lady to her feet. 'Don't know. Just lucky, I guess.'

'Thank the Lord. I'm sorry, young man. I was sure I hadn't loaded that thing.'

'No harm, no foul,' said Brenner.

'Oh well, I suppose there's no way I can't give you a room now,' she said. 'Not after attempting to murder you. That just wouldn't be right. Come on, follow me.'

Brenner picked up the discarded shotgun and followed.

The house was deceptively large inside. Low ceiling, raw logs with mud and straw chinking. Wooden floors covered with a multitude of woven rugs. The front door opened directly into an open living area that comprised a sitting room, dining room and kitchen. In the middle of the room, a fireplace, above it a copper cowl and chimney.

Miss Becket walked through the living area and opened a door on the far side. This led through to a corridor. As she walked down she gestured at the doors.

'This is my room. This one here is a study. Another room, no bed in at the moment. And this one,' she said, stopping outside a door at the end of the corridor. 'This is where you will be staying.'

She opened the door and ushered

Brenner in. All the furniture was covered with dust sheets.

A double bed. A sofa. A round table with two chairs. Against the wall a huge wardrobe. Two more doors and a fireplace.

She opened the one door to reveal an ensuite bathroom. Shower, toilet, and basin.

Pointing at a third door, to the left of the wardrobe, she said. 'That leads outside, so you have you own entrance if need be. Bedding is in the wardrobe. The chimney is clean, so you can use the fireplace. I eat breakfast every morning at five thirty. Oats porridge. Same every morning. Lunch, you can make yourself sandwiches. There be cold meats, cheese, and home baked bread. Dinner is served at six. It's stew. Dinner is always stew. So, if you miss it, or you plan on being out that evening, it don't matter none, because you'll just be eating the same stew the next night. That OK with you?'

'That be fine with me, Miss Becket.'

'You can call me Grandma. What you go by?'

'Brenner. Ded Brenner.'

'What sorta name is, Dead?'

'Name my pappy gave me.'

'Well your Pappy got himself a dark sense of humor, weighing down a poor boy with a name like that. I'll call you Brenner.'

'That be fine with me, Grandma.'

'OK, Brenner. You settle in. Tomorrow you can start by stocking up the log store for winter. Then we can take a look at the roof, particularly on the south side of the house. Also, the gutters, Then the fencing at the front of the property. But tonight, you relax. You a drinking man?'

'Sometimes.'

'Well I drink. Every night, half a bottle of Old Crow. You wanna drink, you bring your own, I don't share my liquor. You smoke?'

'Yes, Grandma.'

'Good. I smoke as well. Pipe by choice but anything will do. Likewise, I don't share my baccy. Make sure you have your own. Now you can sit in your own room, or you can join me in the sitting room, don't make no difference to me. I don't watch television, but I am partial to the radio. I listen to talk and jazz. You don't like it, that be your problem.' The old lady held her hand out. 'Deal?'

Brenner nodded and shook her hand. 'Deal.'

Chapter 5

Kon Yu-Lueng, or Big Yu as he was known in the trade, had just turned sixty-nine years old. He did not celebrate. In fact, he did not even acknowledge the date in any way. To him, one day was much like another. Births, deaths, holidays, or anniversaries did not feature on Big Yu's calendar.

Except for one date. The thirtieth of April. Specifically, the thirtieth of April nineteen sixty-five.

That particular day was held in reverence and respected every year with a minute of silence and a toast of Vietnamese rice liquor. A cloudy, foul tasting distillation that reminded him of his youth. And the war. Friends lost, enemies killed. From the age of thirteen to nineteen he had fought the Americans. Until the final victory on the thirtieth of April, nineteen sixty-five.

After the war had ended, Big Yu had

found himself unemployed and destitute. His family and friends had all been killed. So, he joined a criminal gang run by the notorious, Nam Cam, also known as the Godfather of Vietnam.

With his penchant for violence, his quick mind and his veteran experience, Big Yu had risen through the ranks to become Nam Cam's right-hand man. However, after a series of catastrophic mistakes, Nam Cam and his entire gang had been caught by the Vietnamese police and either sentenced to death or incarcerated for life.

Big Yu was the only upper echelon member to escape.

For the next few years he had tried to rise again but to no avail. The rival gangs had distributed the vacated turf amongst themselves, and Big Yu was declared *persona non-gratia* in the Vietnamese criminal hierarchies.

But not one to ever give up, eventually Big Yu had approached Dung Ha, the Black Widow. She was the new power in charge of the gangs and all control emanated from her throne.

Big Yu had made her a proposal. That he left Vietnam and relocate to either

Australia, America, or Canada. Then, via Dung Ha's contacts, he would become the main pipeline for drugs into the west. Particularly for Fentanyl, a new drug over two hundred times stronger than morphine.

After a protracted negotiation, Dung Ha had agreed that he move to Canada. It was easier for them to get the product into the vast, nearly empty, country and it gave almost unfettered access to North America.

That had been three years ago and now Big Yu was in control of the biggest drug network in Canada and one of the largest in the world.

But still he had people who thought they were shrewder than he.

He stood from his chair and walked across the room to stand in front of the four men who were kneeling on the floor, hands zip-tied behind their backs.

Contrary to his nickname, Big Yu was not a large man. Five seven, slight of build. Dark gray hair swept back to reveal a large forehead. Bold eyebrows. A salt and pepper mustache and goatee beard, styled in the manner of his hero, Ho Chi Minh.

The men kneeling on the floor were, however, all large. WWF large. A size that spoke intimately of high protein diets and copious amounts of steroids. They were all dressed in a similar fashion. Jeans, t-shirts, leather jackets. Emblazoned on the backs of the jackets 'Lumberjacks MC' and an embroidered depiction of a flaming wood axe.

On either side of the bound prisoners stood two more men. Both of obvious Vietnamese extraction. They were dressed in loose fitting linen suits. Dark blue. No neckties. They wore sunglasses even though they were inside.

Big Yu shook his head and sighed. A father disappointed with his children. Exasperated more than angry.

'Did you think I would not find out?' he asked.

No one answered.

'You.' He laid his hand on one of the giant's shoulders. 'Stand.'

The man stood, eyes cast downwards.

'Carl. Did you think I would not discover your thievery?'

'Sorry, boss.'

Big Yu shook his head again. 'Apologies do not change facts,' he said. 'I have treated you with respect and you have spurned that respect and returned it with contempt. What have you got to say for yourself?'

'I made a mistake, boss. Please forgive me. It won't happen again. I swear.'

Big Yu didn't answer for a while, drawing out the moment.

Then he smiled. 'I forgive you, Carl,' he said. 'Even though I should not. But I have always been fond of you.'

Carl smiled back. Tentatively. 'Thank you, boss,' he whispered. 'You won't regret it.'

Big Yu placed his hand on Carl's shoulder again.

Then, with a convulsive strike, he struck sideways, driving his hooked fingers through the giant's esophagus, tearing out his throat, his voice box, and his arteries. The Vietnamese martial art of Vovinam.

He stepped back quickly so as to avoid the spray of arterial blood arcing across the room.

'I forgive you,' he said again. 'But I cannot let you live.'

He gestured to one of the Vietnamese men who drew a pistol and quickly shot the remaining three men in the backs of their heads.

'Get this mess cleaned up,' commanded Big Yu as he left the room. 'And find out how much product these idiots stole. We have an American shipment coming up soon and we cannot afford to be short.'

CHAPTER 6

Brenner sized up the mountain of wood that needed to be split and stacked into cords. Logs that had been chain sawed into two-foot lengths and piled high to dry during the summer months.

He laid one of the logs on the chopping stone, heft the old felling axe and swung hard.

Too hard.

The blade smashed through the log like it was made from *papier-mâché*, splintering the wood into at least twenty pieces, and splitting the rock beneath it.

The big man frowned at his lack of finesse as he checked the axe, relieved to find the ancient hickory shaft and solid steel head was still intact.

Taking more care, he placed another log on the stone, lined it up and took a slow, lazy swing at it. This time it split evenly down the middle. Brenner nodded his approval and struck again, working his way around the log until he had split it into six equal pieces.

He worked methodically all morning, splitting and stacking. By the time lunch came he had worked his way through over five tons of wood.

He buried the axe in a log to protect the blade and headed for the kitchen to make himself something to eat. But when he got there, Grandma had already fixed him a platter of sandwiches. Ham and cheese on doorstep thick slices of freshly baked white bread. To drink, two pints of home brewed ginger beer.

Brenner thanked her and sat at the kitchen table to eat.

She sat opposite him in silence for a while. Then she fixed herself a pipe of tobacco, rubbing the raw baccy and packing it into the bowl with deft fingers. Finally, she lit up using a Zippo pipe lighter.

Brenner concentrated on getting food inside him to replace the vast amounts of energy he had used that morning.

'An average man can cut and stack around half a cord an hour,' said Grandma, as she puffed at her pipe. 'A professional lumberjack twice that. You just cut and stacked ten cords in five hours. That's not possible.'

Brenner said nothing.

'Just saying,' said Grandma. 'You better watch the rate you work unless you want tongues to wag. Your secret's safe with me but be careful with anybody else.'

'I ain't got no secrets, Grandma,' said Brenner.

The old lady chuckled. A dry, rasping cough of amusement. 'Me either,' she said. 'Just saying, that's all.'

The big man downed the last of his ginger beer and headed back to the woodpile.

He worked until sunset. Another five hours. Heeding Grandma's advice he cut and stacked a mere two more cords of wood. A satisfyingly human amount.

CHAPTER 7

It was Friday night and Busby's was filling up fast.

Brenner sat at a small table in the corner eating a steak, a welcome change from Grandma's eternal mystery-meat stew.

He had been in Backlash for two weeks now. And this was the second Friday night. He also came to the diner-come-entertainment-center every Wednesday. Rib night, all you could eat for under ten dollars. Brenner never actually ate his fill. He considered that unfair. After all, why bankrupt a place merely because you could eat more in a sitting than six average men combined.

And, truth be told, now he no longer assumed his Wolf or Wolfman mode, his appetite had dropped substantially. Human forms take a lot less protein to sustain them than superhuman ones.

And for the first time in many years, people had started to greet him. By name.

'Good afternoon, Brenner.'
'Nice to see you, big man.'
'Hello, Brenner. How are you?'
And he greeted them back with a smile. A nod of the head. A word or two.

Like a normal human being. Just a man going about his business. Fixing fences, chopping normal quantities of wood, doing his chores.

No death. No killing.

No retribution.

Perhaps it would be exaggerating to say he was happy … but he wasn't unhappy. And for Brenner, that was the best he could have hoped for after the last fifty years.

'More coffee, big man?' asked Debra.

Brenner smiled and shook his head. 'Think I'll go for a beer, Debra,' he answered. 'Anything domestic.'

She smiled back. 'Sure thing.'

Brenner liked the waitress. Her personal life, which she told everyone about, was a disaster area. Failed love affairs, illegitimate children, estranged family members. But her heart was in the right place and she was unfailingly upbeat.

Of late she had taken to adding false

eyelashes to her raft of makeup, gluing them on with the same cheerful abandon she applied the rest of it. One was always slightly lower than the other, giving her the appearance of a recovering stroke victim. But what would have turned anyone else into a figure of ridicule just became endearing on Debra.

She had flirted heavily with Brenner for the first few days but, when he returned her advances with mere smiling politeness, she had turned her sights elsewhere with no animosity, merely a change of target.

She returned a minute later with a Bud and a smile.

'Thanks,' said Brenner. 'Tell me, Debra, where is Sheriff Colson? I'd like to buy the man a beer.'

Debra stared at Brenner for a few seconds and her smile dropped. 'It's the end of the month,' she said.

'So?'

She shook her head. 'The sheriff don't venture out on the last day of the month.'

She turned and walked away, heading back to the kitchen.

Brenner sat and sipped his beer, wondering what the hell Debra was going on about. Was it some kinda small town tradition? No sheriff Fridays, or something equally obscure.

He finished his beer and waited for Debra to come back to his section, so he could order another. But it soon became obvious she was avoiding him. He was about to stand up and holler for her when he heard it.

The unmistakable sound. And not just one or two of them. At least fifteen. Maybe more.

Motorbikes.

More specifically – Harley's.

He glanced around him and saw everyone else had heard the approaching motorbikes. They could hardly not. The ground was starting to shake, windows rattling in their frames and glasses jiggling on the tables.

But no one reacted. No one even looked up from their meals. Or their beers. Or their conversations.

Ostriches with their heads planted firmly in the sand.

Brenner heard the bikes stop outside the diner. Then, as one, they revved three times and cut out.

Relative silence.

Still no one looked up.

The door opened, and the bikers filed in.

Beards and boots and chains and leather.

Black jackets with their patch emblazoned on the back.

'Lumberjacks MC'

And still no one looked up.

There were twenty-two of them and they filled the place. All large men. Almost cartoonlike. Hours of pumping iron, force-feeding themselves protein, and injecting industrial quantities of steroids.

A man Brenner hadn't seen before appeared behind the bar, entering from a back door. He nodded at the bikers in general then addressed one of them personally. The biggest one.

Six five, three hundred twenty pounds plus. Short black hair and a beard down to his chest. He was toting a large black suitcase.

'Floyd. Glad to see you made it without incident,' the man behind the bar said.

'Well, why wouldn't I, Busby?'

'No reason. Just glad to see you. What

can I get the boys to drink?'

'Same as always. Jack. Bottles.'

Busby nodded then hauled a couple of cases out from under the bar, placing them on the countertop. A few of the bikers came forward and ripped them open.

With whoops of glee they distributed the whisky amongst the group.

Floyd picked the suitcase up and banged it down on the bar. 'Same quantity as last time,' he said.

Busby nodded, took the suitcase off, and replaced it with a smaller one of his own.

'Do I need to count it?' asked Floyd.

Busby shook his head. 'It's all there.'

Brenner sat still. He couldn't believe what he was seeing. In open view of everyone in the place, the bikers were conducting what was obviously some sort of drug deal. The wolf inside of him grunted but Brenner forced it down. He needed to know more about what was going on here before he intervened.

And also, it was nothing to do with him. He was merely a bystander. The new improved Brenner.

No wolf.

No intervention.

Not. His. Problem.

Floyd grabbed a bottle of Jack then turned to survey the room.

Everyone looked down. Avoiding eye contact.

Apart from Brenner, whose chemical makeup was such that, even if he had wanted to, he wouldn't cower.

Floyd walked over to the table, banged his bottle down and sat opposite Brenner.

'You got a problem, boy?' he asked.

Brenner shook his head. 'No problem. Just having a quiet beer. That's all.'

'Ain't seen you before,' continued Floyd. 'You new here?'

Brenner nodded.

'That your rat bike outside?'

Again, the big man affirmed.

'It's a piece of shit,' stated Floyd.

Brenner smiled. 'Gets me where I'm going.'

Floyd held out his bottle of Jack. 'Here, have a drink with me.'

Brenner shook his head. 'No thanks. I was about to leave. Early start tomorrow.'

'I insist.'

Brenner stood, turned, and headed for

the door.

Floyd gestured to a group of his men and they moved to stand in front of Brenner. Cutting off his exit. A wall of muscle.

The wolf growled.

'Excuse me,' said Brenner.

One of the men shook his head. 'Boss wants to drink with you. So, I advise you to do as you're told.'

'*Kill them,*' whispered the wolf.

Brenner held his hands up. 'I'm not looking for trouble, gentlemen,' he said. 'Just going home. This is none of my business, whatever this is.'

The man put his hand on Brenner's chest and pushed him.

It was like pushing a wall. Brenner didn't budge, and the surprise registered on the biker's face.

'*Change,*' said the wolf. '*Change and kill them all. Kill Floyd. Kill the bikers. Kill the town for their cowardice.*'

Brenner grabbed his head and squeezed. 'No,' he said aloud to himself.

'Hey look it,' said Floyd. 'Looks like we got ourselves a bit of a retard here. Talking to himself. What are you? Rain

Man?'

The bikers laughed.

The townsfolk kept their heads down.

'*Raze the town to the ground,*' shouted the wolf in Brenner's mind. '*Destroy all that comes before you. Do it.*'

'No,' yelled Brenner out aloud. 'I don't need you. I can do this myself.'

'What the fuck are you going on about?' asked the biker in front of Brenner.

Brenner stared at him, breathing hard as he tried desperately to control the beast. 'I. Am. Human,' he growled.

And he punched the man in the chest.

The blow sounded like an axe chopping wet wood. The three-hundred-pound man took off like someone had tied a rope to him and attached it to a dragster. He smashed into the door some twelve feet away and slumped to the floor, blood trickling from his nose and ears.

'I am human,' shouted Brenner as he leapt forward, grabbing the next biker, and pulling him into a vicious headbutt that smeared the man's nose across his face.

'Get him,' yelled Floyd.

And, as one, the bikers waded into battle. Feet, fists, chains, and knuckle dusters.

There were twenty-two of them. But by the time they had smashed Brenner to the floor there were only twelve left upright.

As the big man fell, the bikers really brought their boots into play. Stamping and kicking him. The sound of his bones breaking was easily audible above the sound of his flesh being struck.

Blood flowed from numerous cuts on his body, his face, and his head.

He no longer reacted to the punishment he was getting dealt. His body limp. Accepting.

It was obvious to all he was close to death. It was also plain the bikers were not going to stop until he was all the way there.

Then the sound of a shotgun blast rent the air, followed immediately by the sound of another round being racked into the chamber.

'Stop,' shouted Sheriff Colson.

The bikers stopped, and Floyd walked over to stand in front of the sheriff. A sneer on his face. 'Just what the fuck do you think you're doing, old man. We have an agreement.'

'Yes, we do,' agreed Colson. 'But that agreement never included murder.'

Floyd eyeballed the sheriff for a few seconds then burst out laughing. 'Yeah. Whatever, old man. He's probably already dead. We were finished teaching him a lesson anyways. Come on boys,' he continued. 'Let's get to drinking. Oh, and Sheriff, rustle up the doctor and send him over here. That psycho busted up a few of my boys real good.'

Colson nodded then went over to Brenner and knelt beside him, laying his hand on his neck to feel his pulse. It was surprisingly strong. He sensed someone else beside him and he looked up to see Debra,

'Can I help, Sheriff?' she asked.

Colson nodded. 'Help me get him to the car. He's been beat up bad. I'd like the doc to see him before he comes here to sort out this scum.'

Brenner was heavy, but both Colson and Debra were in good shape and, although Brenner was out, he wasn't the absolute dead weight Colson expected him to be. By the time they got him to the patrol car, his feet were actually moving of their own accord.

The sheriff opened the back door and started to maneuver Brenner in, but the big man resisted.

'Come on,' said Colson. 'Quit struggling. We're just gonna take you to the doc. Get you sorted out.'

Brenner shook his head. 'No. I'm fine.'

'Don't be stupid,' said Debra. 'You are not fine. You've got broken bones that will need setting, cuts that need stitching. Concussion. Who knows what else? One of your ribs might even have punctured a lung. Please, Brenner. Stop fighting us.'

The big man stood, and both Debra and Colson gasped in disbelief.

His face and clothes were still drenched in blood, but his eyes were no longer swollen shut. In fact, the cuts on his face were now only closed dark red scars.

'I'm fine,' he said.

'But, how?' asked Colson.

Brenner shrugged. 'Thanks for the save, Sheriff,' he said. 'Looks like they were definitely getting the better of me before you arrived.'

'Well, there were twenty of them,' said Colson.

'Twenty-two, actually,' said Brenner. 'But I got about half of them before I went down. Look, Sheriff, I'm going back to Grandma's, get some rest. If the biker boys ask where I am, tell them I'm in a coma or something. After the hurt I put on them, they aren't going to be happy if they think I'm up and walking about.'

Colson nodded his acceptance of Brenner's advice. 'Sure thing, Brenner. I'll tell them you're at death's door and I put your bike in the pound.'

'Good. Then tomorrow, after these idiots have gone, you and I are gonna have ourselves a long chat.'

Colson nodded. His expression contrite.

As Brenner turned to his Harley, Debra grabbed his arm. 'What are you?' she asked.

An expression of anger flitted cross the big man's face. 'I am human. Just like you.'

Then he mounted his bike and rode off into the night.

'Sure,' whispered Debra to herself. 'And I'm Marilyn Monroe.'

CHAPTER 8

The next night was a full moon. Brenner went deep into the forest, carrying his length of chain and returned early the next morning to Grandma's house.

Then he showered, ate his bowl of oats porridge, and informed Grandma he was going into town to see the sheriff.

Brenner noted the white Crown Victoria was parked outside the sheriff's office, so he parked outside and walked in. A common entrance served both courthouse and sheriff's office. Brenner entered and turned left.

The door opened to reveal a charge desk and waiting area. Behind the charge desk and open archway showed two empty desks with chairs. Behind that, the door to the sheriff's office itself. It was open. The place had obviously been designed for a much larger force but had just as obviously never been used.

Colson sat at his desk, staring blankly

into space. No paperwork in front of him. A laptop, closed. A single ballpoint pen and a glass paperweight. The paperweight had been cast around a brass reproduction of Lincoln. Inscribed on the glass, "*Nearly all men can stand adversity, but if you want to test a man's character, give him power.*"

He did a double take as Brenner's presence jogged him out of his reverie.

'Hey, big man,' he greeted.

Brenner nodded, pulled up a chair and sat. Both men sat in silence for a good few minutes.

Finally, Colson spoke. 'Our helicopter went down just off hill 561 in Khe Sanh, April, nineteen sixty-seven. Burst into flames as we hit. I managed to get the pilot, copilot, and gunner out. Lost three men. Flames just got too hot. Ammo started cooking off. I tried, God knows.'

The sheriff took out a pack of smokes. Offered. Brenner accepted. Colson lit for both of them. Smoking in a government building. His town. His laws.

'Managed to radio for evac but the area had gone to shit. Told me they couldn't get a bird near us for three hours. Said we had to hang in there. So, I strung up some IVs. Made the boys as comfortable as I could. And that's when the gook patrol found us.'

The sheriff leaned back in his seat, his eyes were unfocused. He wasn't looking at the cheap wood paneling. The map of the United Sates. The blue and gold flag with the words, *Oro y Plata* embroidered on it.

Instead he saw the jungle. Green and verdant and terrifying. The black smoke and flames from the downed Huey. The blood and the death.

And the enemy, with their black shirts and brown woolen pants and AK47s.

'I was the only one fit enough to hold a weapon. I had set up an M60 with six belts of ammo, also my M16 and my Colt .45.

'When the bird finally got to get us, I was down to my last magazine in the .45. Been shot twice. Left leg and left shoulder. Had iced nine gooks and hadn't lost one of my men. The Huey sent the slants packing, took us back to base.

'Two months later, they gave me the silver star.'

Brenner didn't respond. He had three silver stars and a navy cross. But that had happened long ago in a life that no longer existed to him.

Colson lit another cigarette. Then he turned to face Brenner.

'I'm not a coward,' he said quietly.

'Are they dealing drugs?' asked Brenner.

The sheriff nodded.

'Are they paying you?'

Colson shook his head. 'I'm not corrupt. Whatever you might think of me.'

'Never said that you were, Sheriff,' answered Brenner. 'So, what's the deal then?'

'It started a couple of years back,' said Colson. 'A bunch of bikers rode into town, Lumberjacks MC. They went straight into Busby's and after a few hours of hard drinking, started to kick up a ruckus. I went on over and asked them to settle down or leave. Obviously, they took umbrage. Told me to go fuck myself.

'I drew down on them, marched them to their bikes and told them to leave and never come back. They laughed but complied. But, just before they rode off, the one asked where my deputies were. I didn't answer. Then he shook his head and laughed even harder. *"You ain't got none,"* he said. "*This one-horse town is also a one sheriff town.*" Then he pointed his hand at me like a pistol, cocked his thumb and went, "B*ang. We'll be coming back, old man,*" he said, "*And next time, no Mister nice guy*." Then they rode off.'

Colson lit two more cigarettes. Proffered one to Brenner.

'Two weeks later they returned. Except this time there were fifty of them. Most on bikes, but also a Range Rover with four Asian men in. The went to the bar, kicked everyone else out and sent for me. Can't deny, I was crapping myself. Thought it was the end for sure. Payback time for Sheriff Colson.'

'But you still went?' asked Brenner.

Colson shrugged. 'What else could I do. If I'd ignored them, who knows how they would have reacted? Shot up the town? Killed some innocent to prove a point? No, I had to go. So, I saddled up and went to take my medicine.'

The sheriff stood and went over to a coffee table at the side of the office. A Bunn flask stood on a heater. Half full. Brenner could smell it from where he sat. Strong and bitter. Colson didn't offer, he simply filled two mugs, handed one to the big man and sat again.

'Long story short,' continued the sheriff. 'They took me by surprise. There was no violence apart from what was implied. Turns out the Asian dudes where from Vietnam. The bikers, Lumberjacks MC, were from Canada. The one Vietnamese dude was in charge. Kon Yu-Lueng, or Big Yu. My sorta age. Fought against us, back in the day. Scary motherfucker. They all had T T T T tattooed on their knuckles. Not sure what that meant…?

'Thoung, Tien, Tu, Toi. Love, money, prison, crime,' interrupted Brenner. 'Bad boys. Ex-street-gang that made good. Started back when we were there. There's no posturing or bullshit with them. They strike hard and fast, no mercy.'

'How you know about them?' asked the sheriff.

Brenner took a sip of his coffee. Didn't answer.

Colson shook his head and continued. 'Anyways, this Big Yu fella tells me it's my lucky day. Says I no longer have to worry about my retirement because he is gonna make me a wealthy man. His plan is, the biker boys bring his shit across the border, using the back routes and forest tracks. Then they deliver it to a contact of theirs in town. This contact distributes the shit to the drivers from the saw mills who then distribute it across the country.

'Tells me like it's a done deal. And, as it happens, it was. Turns out they had already put all the steps in place over the last few weeks. I was just too fucking dozy to see it. So, the only thing left was for me to turn my head the other way, they give me a shit house full of cash every month, and everyone was happy.'

'So, you agreed,' said Brenner.

Colson shook his head as he stood. He untucked the front of his shirt and pulled it up to expose his belly. Brenner glanced down to see two small puckered wounds. About the size a .38 slug would make.

'I told them to go screw themselves.'

'They shot you?'

Colson chuckled. 'Just like that. Big Yu. No warning, no preamble. Just pulled the midnight special out and cranked off a couple of rounds. Knew what he was doing as well. Missed all the major organs. Hurt like a son of a bitch.'

Colson turned around to show Brenner the exit wounds. 'Full metal jacket. No expansion. Through and through. Good shooting.'

'A lesson,' said Brenner. 'What then?'

'One of the other Viet Cong patched me up. Did a real good job. Obviously, a doctor or paramedic of some sort. Then Big Yu told me how it would go down. His boys would pitch up on the last day of every month. The transactions would take place. Mainly Fentanyl, some morphine, some coke. I would ignore them. They would leave a wad of cash for me and that was that. I told them to take their wad of cash and stuff it up their own asses. For some reason they found that funny. Then they left.

'Afterwards, Busby Jackson, the bar owner, came up to me and apologized. Said he didn't know they were going to shoot me. Said he thought he was doing me a favor. Getting me some money for my retirement. Turns out Busby was the one who had put the whole plan in motion. Contacted the Lumberjacks. I ran a check on him. Turns out he did a load of hard time before he came out here. Should have known. Too fucking old for this job.'

'What about calling in the DEA?'

Colson laughed. 'Yeah, sure. By the time they get here we'll all be extinct. Big Yu has contacts everywhere, you think I didn't check him out big time? He'd know we called them in and he'd kill us all. No, it is what it is now. No one gets hurt. I look away. Everyone wins.'

'Except you,' noted Brenner.

Colson nodded. 'Except me.'

'And the over fifty thousand people who die from drug related causes,' added Brenner. 'The majority of which is Fentanyl. Don't forget about them.'

Colson didn't speak.

Brenner stood and left, mounting his Harley, and cruising slowly out of town. When he passed Busby's, he glanced at the window. Normally it was impossible to see inside due to the dirt, condensation, and reflection. But today was different. Today it was like looking at an HD TV. Three men sat at the bar. Two tables in the middle of the room were full, four covers each.

And in the far corner of the

establishment, seated at a table Brenner had never noticed before, were two old men.

Both were dark-skinned with long, gray hair and blue eyes. Bushy gray beards, semiformal clothing. Open-necked white shirts, dark suits, and patent leather shoes. Their clothes were neat and clean, but so threadbare you could almost pick out the individual strands of the weave.

As Brenner saw them they raised their glasses to him and grinned.

The big man slammed on his brakes and slew to a stop. Kicking down his stand he jumped off the bike and strode into the diner. As he entered he blinked a few times, waiting for his eyesight to adjust from the outside glare to the inside shadow.

Before he could look, Debra came over and put her hand on his shoulder. 'Hey, big man,' she said. 'Looks like you're all recovered. That's fine. What can I do you for?'

'Two old men,' snapped Brenner, as he peered into the gloomy corner.

'Oh yes,' said Debra. 'They're over there.' She pointed to the corner then did a double take. 'Oh,' she exclaimed. 'They're gone. Sorry, Brenner, I didn't see them go.'

Brenner walked over to the corer. There was no sign of Mister Bolin nor Mister Reeves. In fact, there wasn't even a table in the corner.

'When did they get here?' he asked Debra.

She looked puzzled. 'Who?' she asked.

'The two old men.'

'What old men?'

Brenner chuckled humorlessly. 'Typical,' he said. 'Son of a bitch. No ways. I don't care if they're watching, I don't want to get involved. I *won't* get involved. Fuck them.'

Debra frowned concernedly. 'Hey, big man,' she said. 'Are you OK? Maybe still a bit punchy from before?'

Brenner gave her a tight grin. 'Yeah, maybe,' he admitted. 'Think I'll go home. Lie down a bit.'

Debra watched him go, oblivious to the one false eyelash that had escaped the confines of her eyelid and was busy heading south to her chin, crawling down her face like a caterpillar.

Then she turned back to check on her customers.

CHAPTER 9

The first snows fell that afternoon as Brenner was cutting back brush from the perimeter, clearing the tracks and the fence line.

He called it a day early, went back inside, brewed himself a coffee, and joined Grandma in front of the fire. He watched the ancient woman pack herself a pipe and light up. Her movements still precise and economical despite her age. He wondered how old she actually was.

'How long you been living here, Grandma?' he asked, reckoning to subtly figure her age by asking a series of questions.

'You wanna know how old I am, don't you?' replied Grandma.

Brenner shook his head and she cackled.

'Yes, you do,' she continued. 'Don't lie to Grandma. Figured it's rude to ask outright so you'd do the whole detective thing instead. Well that's just as rude.'

'Sorry, Grandma.'

She waved her pipe at him. 'Only joshing. When you get to my age you don't care about such stuff. To tell you the honest truth, I'm not so sure how old I am. I stopped counting the birthdays when I hit a hundred and twenty. And that was some time ago. Way before Sheriff Colson got here, and he's been around for over thirty years.'

'That's impossible,' responded Brenner.

'Of course it is,' agreed Grandma. 'And how old you be?'

'Umm ... twenty something. I forget.'

'You forget because it's bullshit, boy. You ain't no twenty something. You's in your sixties at least. Maybe seventies even. Don't bullshit Grandma, it ain't polite.'

'Don't be silly, Grandma,' argued Brenner. 'Do I look seventy?'

The old lady nodded. 'Yep. If you know how to look. A fella don't get eyes like that from twenty years of drifting. No, a fella gets eyes like you when he's been through a world of hurt and back. And that takes time. Sixty years at least, there ain't no short cuts. Gotta live it, boy.'

Brenner finished his coffee and lit a cigarette.

'You fight in 'Nam?' asked Grandma.

The big man nodded.

'Same as Colson,' continued Grandma. 'You know, boy, he ain't no coward.'

'Never said he was,' responded Brenner.

'He just don't know what to do,' said Grandma. 'It's overwhelming.'

Neither of them spoke for a few minutes as they simply sat and watched the flames.

Then Grandma said. 'So, what you going to do about the problems?'

The big man shook his head. 'Not my problems,' he answered. 'I can't afford to get involved in this type of shit anymore.'

'Kill them all,' said the wolf. *'Track them to their den and exterminate them.'*

Brenner lit another cigarette. His hand shook slightly as he did so.

Later that evening they had stew. Then Brenner went and lay down, staring at the ceiling until he finally fell into a fitful slumber just before sunrise.

Chapter 10

Brenner rose before first light every day and worked until sunset. It snowed most days. Light but chilly.

He finished repairing the fencing. Replaced every worn shingle on the roof, refilled the log chinking and painted every surface that needed painting.

He also chopped and stacked even more wood. Enough for a small village.

At night he would sit with Grandma and smoke cigarettes and drink Jack. They would listen to old school jazz and talk radio. People complaining about the millennials. How to cook turkey without drying it out. Home remedies for gout. How to clean your kitchen pots using sand. Endless, mindless drivel, interrupted by advertisements for hemorrhoid creams and denture glues and funeral insurance.

Normal.

Human.

He didn't visit town. Not once. He

didn't want to see the sheriff. The people. It was not his problem. He was Ded Brenner and he worked for Grandma and he was a regular, everyday person.

No monsters here.

Three days before the end of the month, the full moon rose again, and Brenner went out into the forest with his chain and his padlock.

The next morning Grandma served him his oats porridge.

When he had finished, he stood, thanked her, and headed for his room. As he got to the door she called out to him.

'Brenner,' she said. 'You can't run forever. Sometime, you gonna have to turn and face your problems. However bad they might be.'

The big man didn't answer. But he knew she was right.

CHAPTER 11

Solomon leaned back in his chair, steepled his fingers and thought. He had pulled out all the stops to track Brenner down. Normally, despite the big man always trying to stay under the radar, it was relatively easy to get a bead on him.

His moral code sank him every time. Brenner would see an injustice and couldn't stop himself intervening. Then all Solomon would need, was to hear a report, rumor, or story via the grapevine, that mentioned Brenner's MO. A single man beating the crap out of thirty people. A murderer or gangster found with their limbs torn off. Buildings destroyed, whole areas laid waste.

Yep, Brenner was a weapon of mass destruction and hence was pretty easy to find if you knew what you were looking for. Once you found him, well, that was a different story. Easy to find, but incredibly difficult to keep.

For the last two months, however, Solomon's network of informants had heard nothing. Nada.

Solomon was starting to wonder if the big man had actually left the country. Maybe South America. Canada. Mexico.

The intercom on his desk buzzed to pull him out of his reverie and he pushed the button.

'My office,' commanded the colonel in his usual abrupt fashion.

Solomon didn't bother to reply. He simply obeyed.

A minute later he stood in front of the colonel, standing at ease, hands behind his back, eyes on the wall above his commanding officer. Waiting.

'No sign of Brenner?' asked the colonel.

Solomon shook his head. 'Not hide nor hair, sir. He's gone dark.'

The colonel stood and went to the window, twisting the blind open slightly so he could peer out. The sunlight didn't come anywhere near Solomon.

'We have a bigger problem,' stated the colonel. 'This morning, the *Hyaenidae Sapiens* have escaped. All seven of them.'

'The dog boys?' asked Solomon. 'Shouldn't be a problem. I don't know much about them, sir, but I am sure our normal teams can track them down and bring them back pretty smartly. After all, how dangerous can they be?'

The colonel walked over to his desk, turned his laptop around to face Solomon and hit the enter button. 'This is the CCTV footage of the escape.'

Solomon watched the video clip. Then he frowned. 'Shit.'

'Yes,' agreed the colonel.

'Did that one just bite through the steel bars on his cage?' asked Solomon.

'Two-inch-thick, titanium alloy security bars. Bit through it like cotton candy,' confirmed the colonel.

'And then they smashed through a solid concrete wall,' continued Solomon.

'Steel reinforced concrete. Three feet thick. You couldn't drive an Abrams main battle tank through it,' affirmed the officer.

'I couldn't do that,' admitted Solomon. 'Jesus, even Lenny couldn't have done that.'

There was silence for a while as both men considered the enormity of the situation.

'Could Brenner do that?' asked Solomon, his voice barely above a whisper.

The colonel nodded. 'I'm not sure if he knows he can but, yes. Easily.'

'Where do you think the dog boys are heading?'

'I don't know,' admitted the colonel. 'But we have all our resources on it.'

'What do you want me to do?'

The colonel sighed and massaged his temples with his fingers. It was the first time Solomon had ever seen any emotion other than iron self-control. 'I need you to find Brenner.'

'Really?' asked Solomon in disbelief. 'With these things on the loose, I would think Brenner is no longer a priority.'

The colonel shook his head. 'You don't understand. With these things on the loose, Brenner is now our top priority. According to the boffins, he is most likely the only thing alive that might can stop them. Sergeant Solomon, you need to find him and convince him to help us.'

Solomon didn't respond.

'There is one more thing you need to

know,' added the colonel. 'The subjects we used. The ... volunteers. They were all taken from many walks of life. However, by either chance or genetic disposition it so happens the ones who survived the hybridization, are all from a rabid far right group of neo-Nazis known as, *The Sons of One Eight*. One being the letter A in the alphabet and eight being the letter H. Adolf Hitler.'

'The group of nut cases responsible for the Massachusetts Massacre and the Boston movie house bombings?' asked Solomon.

'The very same,' confirmed the colonel. 'And their Alpha is the same man who was their leader before, one Hans Godling. We have recordings of him advocating race war, massive waves of internal terrorism. Wholesale destruction and anarchy. The boffins have put forward the theory that Godling will attempt to make contact with his movement, re-take control and expand his war. If that happens, God help America. We have no idea how far this psychopath could escalate things, they are extremely well-armed and cash rich. They are also, currently the largest neo-Nazi group in the world with over three hundred registered members.

'And with the pack of *Hyaenidae Sapiens* behind him … just find Brenner. The continued safety of our country depends upon it.'

Sergeant Solomon saluted and left the room.

The colonel sat at his desk, opened his drawer, and took out his pump bottle of hand sanitizer. He stared at it for over a minute then simply let it drop to the floor.

Where was Brenner?

CHAPTER 12

Brenner's superhuman hearing picked up the sound of the gunshots over his wood chopping. Muted by distance. The open boom of a shotgun, followed by the crackle of automatics and semi-autos.

It came from the town.

And it was the last day of the month.

He took a deep breath and swung the axe. It was not his problem. And even if it was, he couldn't afford to intervene. The wolf was too close to the surface. Who knows if he could control it.

Who knows if the town would survive his intervention?

He picked up an armful of wood, stacked it and swung the axe again.

He heard Grandma walk up behind him, but he ignored her, concentrating on the heft and feel of the axe. Solid, rhythmic, safe.

'Debra just phoned,' said the old lady. 'Sheriff Colson made a stand. Told the bikers to leave.'

Brenner swung the axe. Wood split.

'They gunned him down,' continued Grandma.

Brenner stopped and turned to face the old lady.

'I just thought you should know,' she said.

'Is he dead?'

She shrugged. 'Does it matter? It's not your problem.' She turned and shuffled back to the house, dragging her feet in the snow so as not to slip.

The big man stood stock still for a few seconds. Then he put his leather jacket on, walked over to the Harley and slotted the axe into the rifle sling next to the saddle. He fired the machine up and headed for the town.

Grandma watched him go.

Then she smiled.

***

Brenner kicked the stand down and dismounted outside Busby's. As usual, the plate glass window was opaque with condensation and dirt.

On the snow, outside the entrance, a flower of blood stood out against the snow. Lots of blood.

Brenner grabbed the axe, heft it over his shoulder, walked to the entrance, pushed the door open and walked in.

There were at least thirty bikers in the bar. Ten or twelve locals sat huddled in the corner, seated at three tables. Brenner wondered why they came on the last day of the month. Probably inured to things. It was simply life to them. Some days the Lumberjacks MC were there, and some days they weren't. It was like shopping in the Lebanon.

Debra scuttled on over to him, took in the axe and the look in his eyes, and flinched.

'The sheriff?' asked Brenner.

'He's alive,' she answered. 'Just. He's at the doc's. Lost a lot of blood.'

It was obvious she had been weeping. Her makeup was worse than usual, and both of her false eyelashes were attached to her lower jaw.

'Tell the locals to leave,' said Brenner.

Floyd looked up from his drink and saw the big man for the first time. He burst out laughing. 'Hey,' he shouted. 'What's with the axe? You auditioning to be part of the Lumberjacks MC?'

The rest of the bikers joined in the laughter. Beta's barking with their Alpha.

Out of the corner of his eye, Brenner saw Debra herding the locals to a side door. He stood still and waited. As the last one left, he took a few more steps into the room, rolling his shoulders to loosen them up. The room grew quiet.

He looked directly at Floyd.

And he let the Wolf show through his eyes.

Floyd rocked back in his seat. 'Holy shit,' he grunted as he realized he was literally staring into the abyss. 'Kill him,' screamed the biker as he pointed at Brenner with a shaking finger. 'Kill that motherfucker.'

The axe whistled through the air and connected with a wet thud. Floyd's head leapt from his shoulders and struck the far wall.

Then the wolf took over.

Brenner didn't bother to change, he simply let the wolf free. Shots rang out, blades glittered, blood flowed and fountained.

Outside the bar, the locals who had just left, heard the gunshots. And the screaming. And the growling. Like some massive animal had been let loose in the building.

Walls shook as bodies smashed into them. Windows exploded as dismembered limbs came crashing through them.

And, finally, after mere minutes … something howled. Primeval and atavistic, the sound vibrated the windows in the town with its volume. And it reached down deep inside every human's soul and grabbed the most basic part of them that governed their primal thoughts and fears, and it turned it to quivering jelly.

Silence.

Then the door swung open slowly. The locals held their breaths.

Brenner walked out. He was covered in blood from head to foot.

He walked over to his Harley, slid the axe into its sling, mounted and rode off.

***

Seventy-two hours later, Solomon put

the phone down and smiled. 'He's in Montana,' he said to Howard. 'Get the BMW ready. We leave tonight.'

CHAPTER 13

The clan had broken out from the facility at the Bloodborn Project in Maryland at twelve minutes past midnight. Then, under the leadership of their Alpha, now Anubis, once known as Hans Godling, they had left on foot, running together at an average speed of a little over forty miles an hour. This is almost twice the pace of an Olympic sprinter.

Keeping to the backroads and rural areas, the clan ran at that pace for six hours straight. Almost two hundred and fifty miles.

They had stopped once, a few miles outside Laymantown. There they had scaled fence and killed a sheep and two farmhands. The clan had eaten them all. Every last scrap including clothes, fur, and even the grass stained with their blood.

Now they had stopped once again, in the Holston Valley. Another farm. This time they had eschewed the cattle and proceeded straight to the farmhouse. There they killed the farmer, his wife and his two daughters.

Then the clan had eaten their fill.

They were almost a third of the way to their destination. *The Sons of One Eight* HQ in Battelle, Alabama. An abandoned town The Sons had moved into some three years before. Now it had its own power supply, water, and communications. The only road in and out was guarded by a steel gate and the entire town was fenced with guard's towers, trip wires and mines.

The official flag, a copy of Old Glory with the stars replaced by swastikas, flew over the entrance, and all inside wore variants of second world war Nazi uniforms with American and Confederate flags added.

Anubis told the clan to rest. They would continue their journey at first light the next morning. He hoped to be at HQ in two more days.

The four permanent hybrids curled up together in the front room. The permanents stood on their hind legs, a little over six feet tall, massively overdeveloped musculature. But their knees bent backwards like a hyena, so their gait looked slightly awkward. Like an amateur stop-motion film effect.

Their faces were largely human. Particularly their eyes and ears. But their jaws were pure hyena. Large and elongated with black lips and prominent canines. And the massive slabs of jaw muscle covering their head and back, bulged upwards into a hump behind their neck the size of a football.

They stank of wet fur and rotting meat.

Even the three *Hyaenidae Sapiens* that had full control over their metamorphic capabilities displayed the same hunched slab of muscle on their backs. So, Anubis knew, although they passed as full human, there would be Quasimodo references and bell ringing jokes. Until he tore the jokers' heads off.

Satisfied all was going to plan, the Alpha sat on the sofa and went to sleep.

CHAPTER 14

Brenner had been heading towards Canada, riding north towards the West Poplar River Point border entry. But then, a couple of miles before the checkpoint, he pulled the Harley off the main road and onto one of the smaller dirt tracks that ran at a right angle.

He crossed the border seven miles away from West Poplar River Point, avoiding the authorities and any exposure to the fact he had no passport or form of ID.

An hour later he was back on the blacktop and heading for Swift Current, Saskatchewan.

Swift Current was a small town of close to twenty thousand souls. Large airport, good roads, railway links. Because Brenner hadn't merely killed when he had entered Busby's bar in Backlash, he had also questioned. And he had discovered the sleepy town of Swift Current was the head of operations and dwelling place of one

Big Yu. The man in ultimate charge of the Lumberjacks MC and their illegal payloads.

And it was time Swift Current had a clean out.

Apparently, Big Yu lived in a large ecofriendly home outside the town, down the trans-Canada highway about five miles. There were outbuildings, barns, and three more houses plus a large dormitory-style residence. The entire compound was fenced, and a large sign outside said, "Trans Asian Marine – import, export services".

You couldn't miss it.

Brenner rode into town, moving slowly due to the snow on the road, engine barely ticking over as he checked out the lay of the land.

The Lyric theater. A large, ornate court house. The Imperial Hotel. He had been in towns so similar it was almost *deja vu*. Like his life was on some sort of loop where he woke every morning and went out to find someone else's shit to wallow in. Someone else's problems to solve.

Someone else to kill.

He cruised past the Motel 6, the

Comfort Inn, heading towards the less salubrious parts of town. Finally, he spotted a motel that wouldn't ask questions or demand ID. The neon light buzzed its siren call as he parked and walked into the small reception. The place seemed clean enough, the receptionist, a middle-aged man with a bad combover and an unidentifiable piece of vegetation stuck in his front incisors.

Brenner paid in cash for two days, took his key and went to his room to plan the next part of his act of retribution.

And inside him the Wolf growled and threw itself against the bars of his self-imposed cage.

***

Howard had driven for thirty-six hours straight, stopping only to fill up with gas, purchase food, and swallow the odd amphetamine. The trunk of the BMW seven series was full of weapons and serum. Enough serum for almost four weeks. Enough weapons for a major war.

They arrived at Backlash around a half an hour before sunset. Howard parked in the main street and, as per Solomon's instructions took a walk around the town and asked a few questions.

Solomon peered out of the heavily tinted windows at a building called "Busby's" and he started to chuckle. The windows were all boarded up, the door had been hastily nailed back on and the walls had bowed out in places like a hand grenade had gone off inside.

Classic signs of Brenner.

While he was laughing he noticed a woman check out the car then cross the street towards him. Even from a distance, his finely tuned senses could detect her nervousness. It was like she knew who he was.

As she got closer he could see she was middle-aged but dressed a few years too young. A good figure, and a face that would have been attractive but for the fact she looked like a blind person had applied her makeup for her. One of her false eyelashes was actually closer to her eyebrow than her eyelid.

She stopped outside the back window and knocked.

Solomon cracked the window. Enough

for her to see him, but not enough to let any of the fading sunlight in.

'Yes?'

'Are you Sergeant Solomon Hopewell?' she asked.

'Maybe? Who's asking, good lady?'

'Brenner.'

'Well then, yes. I am he.'

'Brenner said when you came I should send you to Grandma Becket's place. It's down the road out of town,' she pointed. 'That way for a couple of miles. First driveway on the right. You can't miss it. He said to be nice.'

'I'm always nice,' said Solomon. 'Well known for it. Will he be there?'

The woman shrugged. 'Don't rightly know, Mister Hopewell. He just told me to give you the instructions.'

Solomon nodded his thanks and flicked the window back up. The woman left and, moments later, Howard got back into the car.

'Who was that?'

'Brenner sent a messenger,' answered Solomon. 'Out of town for a couple of miles. First right. You find anything?'

'Not much,' admitted Howard. 'Not that

they were hiding anything. They just didn't know much. They all knew Brenner, knew he took out an entire motorbike gang, between thirty and forty people. He used an axe. No mention of a Wolfman, or any animal. Oh, apart from the fact he howled. Or, as they all say, they heard something howl. No one knows what it was.'

'He took on over thirty bikers without changing,' mused Solomon. 'Why take the risk? Normally he would just change and fuck the axe. Claws and teeth and casual dismemberment are Brenner's MO. Strange. Maybe this Grandma Becket will shine a light on things. Or maybe Brenner will be there. Although I very much doubt that.'

Mere minutes later, Howard drew up outside Grandma Becket's log cabin. He stepped out and jogged around the back to open the door for Solomon.

The two approached the front door of the house and Solomon knocked.

The door swung open.

'Enter.'

The two men stepped into the room. The door closed behind them, moving of its own accord. But Solomon could feel a small tingle of power as it did so. Like a frisson of static electricity.

An old lady sat on a wingback chair next to a central fireplace. She was smoking a pipe and tendrils of blue smoke wound around her head, untouched by the draft that had blown in when the door opened.

She pointed at the open seats opposite her.

'Sit. Smoke if you want. I won't offer food or drink, as you aren't guests, merely receivers of a message, however, you are welcome to stay a while and ask any questions you want. I cannot guarantee I'll be able to answer them, but you are welcome to ask.'

'You are Grandma Becket?' asked Solomon.

The old lady nodded.

'I am Sergeant Solomon Hopewell,' said the man in black. 'I seek Sergeant Ded Brenner.'

'Why?'

'I need a favor,' admitted Solomon.

'You want to take him back to that unholy prison you call the Bloodborn Project, so you can dissect him,' said

Grandma.

Solomon shook his head. 'No. Not this time.'

'But usually?'

The man in black nodded. 'Usually. This time is different.'

'How?'

So, Solomon told the old lady the entire truth. The hyena men, their escape, the danger. And the fact Brenner was their only hope. Even though what he said was top secret and it was beyond his remit to divulge, he opened up. He didn't know why, it just seemed the correct thing to do.

The old lady stared at him for a while. Then she repacked her pipe, lit it and stared some more. 'You are not an evil man,' she said, eventually.

Solomon raised an eyebrow in response.

Then she looked at Howard. 'You,' she shook her head, 'not so sure about you.'

As always, Howard's expression didn't change. He didn't even bother to look at Grandma. Merely sat at attention in his chair, back upright, eyes straight ahead. Awaiting instructions.

She puffed at her pipe again, staring off into the distance, a look of contemplation on her face. Then she nodded. 'He has gone to a town called Swift Current, Saskatchewan, Canada. Left yesterday. He's going to clear out the source of the trouble this town has been having for the last few years.'

Solomon stood. 'Thank you, ma'am.'

'You going to help him?'

Solomon smiled. 'Unless he has decided to declare war on Canada, he won't need help. However, we will find him and see if we can make his quest a little easier. Then he and I shall have a chat.'

'Good,' said the old lady.

Solomon and Howard left, closing the door behind them.

Grandma leaned back in her chair and listened to the sound of the high-power limousine as it drove off, heading to Canada.

With a sigh, she poured herself a tumbler of whisky, took a sip, then spoke.

'I know you're there. Show yourselves. It's the polite thing to do.'

There was a shimmer of air.

And two old men sat opposite her. Both were dark-skinned with long gray hair and blue eyes. Bushy gray beards, semiformal clothing. Open-necked white shirts, dark suits, and patent leather shoes. Their clothes were neat and clean, but so threadbare you could almost pick out the individual strands of the weave.

They each had a shot glass in their hands. The one raised an empty one to Grandma. An offering.

Grandma snorted her disapproval. 'Away with you,' she snapped. 'You know that I don't drink that shit no more.'

Mister Reeve laughed, and the shot glass disappeared.

'Still interfering?' asked Grandma.

'No,' denied Mister Bolin. 'Simply watching. As always.'

'So, you believe he is the one?' asked the old lady.

Both of the old men flinched. 'We never said that,' answered Mister Reeve.

'Didn't need to,' said Grandma. 'I might be old, and I might no longer play the game, but I am still "she who protects". I may only be a mere *malak* and you may both be *principati,* but these old eyes can still see beyond. And they say that you believe him to be one of the lost Virtues of the Lord.'

'What do you think?' asked Mister Bolin.

Grandma sighed. 'I think that our time has passed. I think that the gods of technology and fame and farce have won. I think that evil has become so bland and unnoticeable, that it has tainted all, and we can no longer fight against it. I believe that we have been forsaken due to our own smug arrogance and conceit. I believe that the Lord no longer cares.'

'You are wrong,' stated Mister Reeve.

'What of the man in black?' asked Grandma.

'He is a mere foot soldier,' replied Mister Bolin.

'Perhaps,' agreed Grandma. 'But perhaps not. The servant. The one who works with him. He is evil. But the man in black … he is a product of the system. It will be interesting to see what he becomes, for, trust me, watchers, he has a role to play. Now go. Give an old lady her privacy and her peace.'

Again, the air shimmered and a far-off sound of a children's choir drifted into hearing.

And they were gone.

Grandma relit her pipe and remembered days gone by. When life had been simpler. As opposed to the unsolvable enigma that it had become.

She smiled. That was Brenner's power. His ability to render all down to black and white. There were no shadows in his life. Things were either right … or they were wrong.

If they were right, then you left them alone. If they were wrong, you fixed them.

That was the power of true simplicity that the modern world had forgotten as it strove to become more sophisticated. Worthier. And at the same time, worthless.

CHAPTER 15

Brenner had cruised around for almost an hour and he could find only one bar that even came close to meeting the criteria that he was searching for. Basically, he was looking for the place where the Lumberjacks MC hung out.

But there was a seeming dearth of biker bars in the town. And even this one, with its broken neon signage that blinked out its name, *Bar None,* wasn't a proper biker joint. Maybe two or three bikes but mainly SUVs. And the bikes weren't even Harleys. Japanese and Italian.

But it was a place to start.

The big man dismounted, walked in, and went straight to the bar. The barman greeted him with a surly nod.

'You serve food?' asked Brenner.

Without speaking, the barman slid a single page menu across. Brenner glance at it then pointed at the house special. 'And two beers,' he added. 'Whatever's local.'

The man pulled two Molson's out of the fridge, opened them, and put them in front of Brenner. He didn't offer a glass and Brenner didn't ask for one. A few minutes later his food arrived. Poutine and a meat pie. Brenner hadn't known exactly what he was ordering and was pleasantly surprised to find that poutine was French fries covered with gravy and cheese curds. The meat pie was also a triumph, full of beef, crispy pastry and loaded with spices. He ate in his usual ravenous manner then ordered another plate of poutine and two more beers.

He thought of lighting up but, after glancing around, he reckoned not. Noticing that even lawless Canadians didn't do things like smoke in public places.

The bar was a fair size. The usual mix of tables and booths. At the far end, a pool table. No juke box but there was music playing. Something generic. Shit.

A few groups. Some single drinkers. At the pool table, a girl and four men. Large. Beards and thick forearms. Not bikers. Brenner could hear that they were speaking French. The girl was small. Red hair, green eyes. Tight jeans and tighter T-shirt that showed off a spectacular figure. Brenner watched her surreptitiously for a while, appreciating the view.

He reckoned that he would have another couple of beers then quiz the bartender as to where he could find the Lumberjacks. But for the next half an hour or so, he was happy to simply sit in the warmth and do nothing.

'Hey, *connard*. You like to look like a pervert at my girl? *Tu m'emmerdes!*'

Brenner snapped out of his reverie to see one of the pool players standing next to him. He was bigger than he had thought. Shading Brenner by a couple of inches and at least twenty pounds.

Brenner held his hand up. 'Sorry, dude,' he said. 'No offense meant. Just admiring the view.'

The girl walked over with the other three men behind her. 'Ah, leave him alone, Felix,' she said. 'No harm in looking.' She pouted at Brenner and winked.

'C'est vraiment un trou de cul, celui-là!' yelled Felix. 'He needs to learn some respect.' He loomed over Brenner. 'What do you say, *fils de pute?*'

Brenner shook his head. What was it with him. It's like he was some sort of asshole magnet. Tie him to a pole and wave him over a crowd and all the assholes would stick to him like shit to a blanket.

'I'm sorry, dude,' he replied. 'I don't understand you, on account of the fact I don't speak dickhead. So why don't you just fuck off and leave me alone?'

Felix smirked. 'Yankee? Well, I think it's time that you learned some manners. In Canada, it is not acceptable to stare like a pervert at someone else's girl.'

The rest of the men crowded forward, surrounding Brenner's barstool. The girl hung back, but it was obvious from her expression that she was enjoying herself. Men fighting over her sullied virtue. A poor man's Helen of Troy. Bargain basement lady in distress.

But Brenner had had enough. He grabbed Felix by the shirt, his hand whipping out faster than a human could register. Then he dragged him in close. Real close, their eyes inches apart.

And the Wolf inside howled and threw itself against its restraints, gnashing and biting. *Kill*, it screamed. *Tear him apart. Do it. Now.*

The blood drained from Felix's face as he saw the beast in Brenner's eyes, and he took an involuntary step backwards, tripping over his own feet and falling to the floor. Then he stood, turned around, and walked slowly to the door on unsteady limbs.

'Hey,' shouted one of the other men. 'What the hell, Felix. You sick or something?'

But Felix didn't answer, he simply grabbed his coat and left.

'Fuck this,' said the man who had shouted at his compadre. 'Looks like it's up to me to teach this *enculé* a lesson.'

And, without warning, he swung a massive overhand at Brenner's head.

There was a blur of movement, a crackle of splintering bone and the man fell to the floor squealing in agony, jagged splinters from both his radius and his ulna poking out through the flesh on his forearm.

His two friends grabbed him under his arms and dragged him from the bar. They didn't even bother to look back. Or check that the girl was following them. It was emergency casevac time at the *Bar None*.

The rest of the patrons at the bar stopped talking for a while but, as soon as they saw that the incident was over, they started up again.

Brenner took a sip of his beer, and noticed that the girl was still standing there.

'Those boys don't never run from nothing,' she said.

Brenner shrugged. 'Well, they can't say that any more, can they?'

'Guess not,' she admitted. 'My name's Romy. You gonna buy me a beer?'

'Sure,' answered Brenner as he gestured to the barman. 'Beer for the lady. Whatever she drinks.'

The barman slid a bottle of Maudite over. Romy toasted Brenner and took a sip as she sat in the barstool next to him.

'What you do to Felix?'

'Nothing.'

'Then why he shit himself like that. Ain't never seen a man so scared. He just turned and walked outta here.'

'Maybe he had to see a man about a dog. Who knows?'

Romy laughed. 'You funny.'

'Hilarious,' agreed the big man.

'What's your name?'

'Ded Brenner.'

'Dead?'

'Yep.'

'I like it,' said Romy. 'You got a place to stay?'

Brenner nodded.

'Close?'

'Yep.'

'You wanna take me back there an' fuck me?'

Brenner nodded. 'Yep.'

Romy giggled. 'Cool. Let's go.'

***

Romy sat on the bed, naked, her breasts uncovered. She was proud of her body, and with good reason. She nibbled on her hair as she watched Brenner walk back from the shower and she marveled at his physique. She was young but, in a town where not a lot happened, she had used sex as her go to source of entertainment and, as such, had seen a lot of men's bodies.

But none like the man standing opposite

her.

Firstly, his body was literally covered in scars, well healed ones but they were nevertheless observable when close up. Secondly, his muscle was so hard it felt like steel. Steel covered with a light coating of rubber. And his obvious strength was both frightening and immensely appealing at the same time. He handled her like she was something fragile and precious he might break by mistake, and that made her feel safe and cherished.

But he was also rough when he needed to be, satisfying the animal-like lust and need that overwhelmed her when they climbed onto the bed. A fever of desire she had never felt before with any other man, or woman. It was as if she were caught in a storm, a force of nature that threatened to engulf her while, at the same time, it had set her free.

And their lovemaking had left her utterly sated and spent.

Flat water after a hurricane.

'Talk to me about the Lumberjacks MC,' said Brenner as he lit a cigarette.

'They don't come into town much anymore,' she answered.

'Anymore?'

'Not since Big Yu settled here. He's a local business man. Not sure what he does but I'm pretty sure it's not all legal. He controls the bikers. Keeps them out of town. He's well respected here, gives money to the church, local clubs, youth movements. I think he's Chinese or something.'

'Vietnamese,' corrected Brenner.

'Same thing,' responded Romy.

'So not,' said Brenner. 'Trust me. Very different.'

Romy shrugged, which did interesting things to her naked breasts and made Brenner lose his focus for a few seconds.

'So where do they hang out then?' asked Brenner.

Big Yu owns a bar out of town. On the highway. Six or seven miles. Got a real stupid name. Something like, mack, stack, rack … something.'

'*Mot! Hai! Ba! Do!*' said Brenner. 'Means, one, two, three, drink. Drinking game they play in 'Nam.'

'Yeah,' agreed Romy. 'That's it. How you know that?'

'I just know shit,' responded Brenner.

Romy stood and started to dress. 'You can't go there,' she said. 'Gotta be invited. Strictly Lumberjack MC. You go there without an invite and you sure gonna suffer something terminal.'

'Whatever,' said Brenner. 'You leaving?'

'Yeah, gotta get home.'

'Need a lift?'

'No. I'm close. Just need to get back before my papa goes mental. Thinks I'm out visiting a girlfriend.'

Brenner raised an eyebrow. 'How old are you?' he asked.

Romy giggled as she put her coat on and opened the door. 'Doesn't really matter, does it? I'm old enough. How old are you?'

She blew him a kiss and closed the door without waiting for an answer.

Brenner lit another cigarette. Then he smiled. She was right. It didn't matter. He was also old enough.

CHAPTER 16

Solomon arrived in Swift Current late morning and had Howard drive them straight to a privately-run boutique hotel on the outskirts of the town. He transferred, under cover, to the reception and hired two rooms.

Then he had slept while Howard went out with specific instructions on what to find, and what to look for in the town.

Howard returned just before twilight and gave his report.

It was as Solomon had suspected. Brenner had been seen cruising the town, but Howard hadn't found where the big man was staying.

The biker gang Brenner had run into in Backlash, frequented a bar out of town that was, to all intents and purposes, a private club house called, *Mot! Hai! Ba! Do!* Howard had taken a drive by the place and noted the place was still standing, no broken windows or smashed doors.

Also, Howard reported there had been no explosions, massive fires or dead bodies found on the streets the night before.

So, Solomon could deduce that, although Brenner was in town, he hadn't yet gone to the bikers' bar although he may have formulated a plan of attack. Solomon laughed. He already knew what Brenner's plan would be. It would be the same plan he always used. Find enemy. Crush enemy. Leave. Fantastic in its essential simplicity.

The two men availed themselves of a splendid meal at the hotel, then they proceeded to the *Mot! Hai! Ba! Do!*

Howard parked outside, and Solomon informed him he should stay in the car.

'No need to make the locals nervous,' chuckled the man in black. 'I'll just go in, order a quiet drink and wait for the big man to arrive.'

'You sure he'll come?' asked Howard.

'Of course,' confirmed Solomon. 'If Brenner is one thing, he's predictable. Well, to a point. He will be here, and sooner rather than later, not being one for procrastination.'

Solomon entered the bar and walked

through to the back, standing in the corner for a while. Simply observing. No one noticed him, because he didn't want to be noticed and, as such, he was merely a darker patch in the shadows. A non-presence.

There were thirty-four men in the bar. No females. Solomon wondered if that was some sort of policy or were the Lumberjacks simply leftovers from a bygone age of pure misogynism. Many of the bikers were armed. Mainly blades, but also a fair smattering of revolvers, pistols, and the odd sawn-off shotgun.

After ten minutes, Solomon got bored, so he decided to order a drink.

Swaggering up to the bar, he banged the surface to get the barman's attention and called out his preference.

'Whisky,' he said. 'Scotch, single malt, no water, no ice.'

The entire bar went as silent as a sleep clinic.

'Who the hell are you?' snapped the barman.

'Names are not important,' replied Solomon. 'All you need to know, is I am the man who ordered a scotch. And I'd like it today, if that's not too much of an imposition, good man.'

'Get the fuck outa my bar,' growled the barman.

Solomon inspected his nails, unperturbed by the barman's demeanor. 'Scotch,' he repeated in a bored voice.

The gang of bikers started to crowd around the man in black, faces leering.

Hey, peon,' said one of them. 'Time you left before we decide to tear you a new asshole. Now, I'm gonna let you go unpunished, because I reckon you just might be a bit simple and you wandered in here by mistake. So, fuck off like a good little retard and we won't hurt you none.'

Solomon eased himself up onto a barstool and turned it to face the crowd, 'Shan't,' he said with a grin.

'Get out,' roared the biker.

'Listen up, easy rider,' answered Solomon. 'I have come to this establishment for a quiet drink and a little light entertainment. And I will not be leaving until I feel like it. Understood?' Then he turned back to the barman. 'If you don't have scotch I suppose that I could be tempted by a shot of dark rum. No ice.

Chop, chop, now, fellow. Time is money and all that.'

The biker who had been talking to Solomon drew a knife. Eight inches of Bowie, and he waved it in front of the man in black. 'Last chance, peon,' he said. 'Then I remove bits of your face.'

Again, Solomon shook his head. 'And miss all the fun?' he asked. 'Not bloody likely.'

'What fun?'

The sound of a Harley approached. It stopped outside. Footsteps moved toward the door.

'That fun,' stated Solomon, pointing at the entrance.

The door burst open. All eyes swiveled to the newcomer.

Six feet five or six, over two hundred and fifty pounds. He wore jeans, a white T-shirt, and a leather coat.

Over his right shoulder he carried an old wood axe.

Then he pulled his lips back in a feral snarl and growled.

'Oh my,' said Solomon. 'What big teeth you have.' And he burst out laughing.

CHAPTER 17

Brenner closed the door behind him then cast his glare over the crowd. 'Anyone who isn't a member of Lumberjacks MC,' he said. 'Get out now while the getting's good.'

'Fuck you,' yelled one of the bikers. 'We're all Lumberjacks.'

'Yeah,' shouted another. 'Lumberjacks until death.'

Brenner nodded. 'Until death, then,' and he swung his axe.

Solomon watched the big man's fighting style with great interest. Normally he didn't have the time to do so, as, normally, he was on the receiving end of whatever Brenner was dishing out. But this time he was merely an interested bystander.

At first glance it appeared Brenner was a simple wrecking machine. All strength, speed, and power with little or no subtlety. But if you watched carefully, you could see a different level emerge. Sure, the overwhelming use of brute force was still there, but it wasn't simply hack and slash. He fought like a Grandmaster plays chess. Always at least three to four moves ahead. Planning as he dealt his cards of death.

And with so many armed assailants attacking at the same time, he needed to be forward thinking.

Solomon noticed the barman bend down and retrieve a pump action shotgun from behind the bar. As he leveled it at Brenner, the man in black casually backhanded him. The blow was so hard it literally tore his head from his shoulders.

Solomon tutted ruefully. 'I suppose that rum is out of the question now?' he enquired to the twitching corpse.

Looking back up at the fight, he saw Brenner's axe had broken and he was starting to get overwhelmed. Because, no matter how fast you are, or how strong, there is a limit to how many well-armed, well trained combatants a single unarmed human can fight at the same time.

Fortunately, Brenner wasn't human.

'Time to go Wolfman,' muttered Solomon to himself.

But Brenner didn't shift. He kept fighting as a human being. But he was slowing down. A knife stuck out of his left shoulder, a savage cut on his forehead kept running into his eyes and a shot from a .38 had hit him in his left thigh, fortunately going straight through without hitting the bone.

There were nine bikers left.

'Change,' shouted Solomon as he stood off his bar stool.

But still, the big man continued fighting in his human form.

Six bikers left.

One of the Lumberjacks swung a chain around his head and connected with Brenner's temple. The big man staggered and slipped down on one knee. As he did so, another biker stabbed him in the chest. It was a small switchblade and didn't penetrate deep enough to do any fatal damage, but it was still a serious wound.

Brenner stood, grabbed the knife wielder, and dragged him into a terminal headbutt. Dropping the body, he spun and latched onto the chain that had struck him in the head. Yanking it hard he pulled the wielder towards him, wrapped the chain around his neck and pulled. Bones grated together and snapped.

Four bikers left.

And now Brenner had a weapon again. He swung the chain around him like a propeller, and when it hit someone it was like they had walked into the path of a wrecking ball.

Two left.

Then one.

None.

The big man dropped the chain, vaulted over the bar, and took down a glass and a bottle of Jamaican rum. He poured. Slid the glass across to Solomon, took a deep swig from the bottle and wiped his mouth with the back of his hand.

'So,' he said, his voice rough with pain. 'What the hell do you want?'

CHAPTER 18

'Home,' growled Anubis as he stood outside the main gates to the town, the newly risen moon behind him.

A spotlight swiveled around from the guard tower next to the gate, pinning to Anubis, formerly Hans Godling.

'This is private property,' shouted the guard. 'You are not welcome. Leave now or face the consequences.'

'Have you lost your mind, storm trooper,' countered Osiris, the clan's beta. 'Do you not recognize your rightful leader, Hans Godling?'

The guard peered down at them, adjusting the spotlight slightly. 'You're not Oberfuhrer Godling. The senior leader is dead. He was taken by the government. Oberfuhrer Johansen is our new senior leader. You're just some random hunchbacked bum. Now get moving before I shoot you.'

'You have until the count of three to

open the gate, stormtrooper,' shouted Osiris. 'After that we will be obliged to use force.'

'Fuck you,' replied the guard. 'On the count of three I'm going to shoot your ass. Now move.'

Anubis beckoned to the four permanents. 'Take the gate down,' he commanded them.

Together, they walked towards the gate, flexing their shoulders as they did so.

The guard, seeing that they were all ignoring his threats, drew a bead on Anubis and pulled the trigger. He was armed with a AR 15, which is basically a civilian version of the military M16. It fires a 5.56mm NATO round. This round is capable of taking out a three-hundred-pound wild boar, or a human at over six hundred yards away. The guard was firing from just over twenty yards. Close to point blank range.

The projectile struck the alpha on his right pectoral muscle, high up on his chest and ricocheted off at an acute angle, leaving a small scorch mark and a tear in his shirt.

Anubis looked up at the guard, smiled

then shook his finger at him.

The guard flinched in disbelief then opened up, pulling the trigger as fast as his finger would allow. The ten-round mag emptied in just over three seconds. Almost every shot struck true, but they didn't even cause Anubis to take a backward step. Instead, they simply served to rile him up.

Then the permanents tore the massive steel gate off its hinges like it was a mere paper facsimile.

The guard stared down at the clan in terror as he realized what he was facing was not human. He desperately stabbed at the panic button mounted on the side of the tower, and the strident call of the alarm added itself to the clamor of the gunshots he had just fired, and the barking and growling and hooting of the things below him.

The tower shuddered, and he looked down to see that two of the things had thrown themselves against it. They repeated this twice more and the structure tumbled to the ground. The last thing the hapless stormtrooper saw, was the gaping maw of some sort of animal as it crunched down on his head.

By now, the noise had attracted scores more people and they came boiling out of the various buildings close to the entrance. The staccato sounds of gunfire filled the night as they competed with the savage growling and giggling of the both the *Hyaenidae Sapiens* and the permanents.

But Anubis was not here to destroy his own movement. He was here to regain control and meld it into the new weapon he was now capable of making it.

He ran and jumped onto the roof of the nearest structure, a shoebox shaped flat roofed storage building. Then he threw his head back and let out a howling scream. The sound sundered the evening air. The sound of darkness. Of unknown things in the night. Of blood and slaughter and malice.

It was the sound of corruption, and it called to the evil ones, like a siren calls a sailor to the rocks.

The gunfire stuttered to a desultory stop.

They turned to listen.

And Anubis spoke to them about what was about to come to pass.

***

A new regime had been put in place.

Jan Johansen, who had risen to leadership when Godling had disappeared, had been summarily executed. Opposition, even in potential, would not be tolerated.

Anubis was once again the Oberfuhrer. Osiris and Set had been officially named as his leutnants, with Osiris being the oberleutnant.

Below him he had restructured the troops. Initially, Seventy-four of them, fifty-five males and nineteen females. Anubis had made them all swear a blood oath to him, cutting the palms of their hands and grasping his to seal the deal. Two men and one woman had refused. Then there were Seventy-one troopers. Fifty-three males and eighteen females.

Everyone was given the rank of Sturmmann, or Stormtrooper, but for two squad leaders who reported directly to his leutnants.

A full week had passed, and the entire movement was arrayed before him now. They wore dark gray jumpsuits, gray baseball caps and black special forces boots. Both caps and shoulders bore the new symbol for the Sons of One Eight. A snarling Hyena above crossed lightning bolts. Underneath, their new motto. The Clan is our Strength.

Anubis' bodyguards, the four permanents, stood behind and to the side. They wore the same jumpsuits, but over that they had long black dusters, complete with a full hood that they wore up, covering their faces in deep shadow. Like all the *Hyaenidae*, their clothes had been substantially tailored to fit the vast humps of muscle that covered their upper backs.

'Stormtroopers,' shouted Anubis. 'The war has begun. A war that will bring the white man to his proper place in America. A war against the Catholics, the Jews, the blacks, and the homosexuals. Foreigners will be expunged from our soil, dissenters and left wing propogandists will be destroyed, and the word of almighty God will prevail over all.'

Behind him one of the permanents rose the Son's flag. The Swastika and Stripes.

And as one, the gathering stared to sing the Horst Wessel song.

Raise the flag.

The ranks tightly closed.
The Son's march with calm ready step.

Anubis let them finish before he continued. 'On this first day of the war, we gather here to plan our next steps. And our next step will be, to acquire more weapons. Real weapons of war, not hunting rifles and semiauto pistols, but SAW machine guns, and mortars and grenade launchers.'

The stormtroopers cheered.

'And we will be getting this equipment from none other than the corrupt, weak, leftist United States Army.'

Osiris rolled down a large map on a stand behind Anubis.

'We will strike here,' said Anubis, pointing at a red circled area on the map. 'This is the National Guard armoury in Marion. Due to budget cuts by the bleeding left liberals, this armoury is marked for closure. A convoy of trucks will be leaving Marion in three days, taking the weapons to the National armoury for safe keeping.' He ran his finger down the map slightly. 'We will hit them here. We will destroy them utterly, leaving no witnesses, and as such, there will be no come back. This is how we will do it …'

CHAPTER 19

A line of smoking M35 two-and-a-half-ton trucks stood scattered along the short stretch of road. At each end of the convoy, a destroyed Humvee, both with their M2 Browning machine guns bent and broken.

Dead bodies and parts thereof lay everywhere.

A group of Navy Seals walked amongst the carnage and the wreckage, weapons hot, ready for anything. And even their battle-hardened faces were pale with shock, such was the severity and wanton barbarity of the attack that had taken place.

A man with sergeant's stripes stood and shook his head in bafflement. 'What the hell were they shooting at?' he asked himself. There was no sign of returned fire, no spent cartridges other than those fired by the convoy. And no sign of any wounded enemy.

And the wounds that the soldiers had suffered were beyond horrific. It was almost as though a great white shark had grown legs and walked amongst them, taking huge bites out of body and equipment alike. None of it made any sense whatsoever.

'Sergeant,' called out one of the Seals. 'Over here.'

The sergeant ran over. Lying on the floor, his pelvis crushed by one of the trucks that had fallen on its side, his right arm almost severed from his torso, lay a man. It was beyond belief that he was still alive.

A medic ran over and started to rip open his kit, pulling out bomb bandages and drips. Working fast and efficiently but ultimately knowing it was a losing battle.

'Hang in there, son,' said the sergeant. 'We'll get you home. Did you see who did this?'

The man nodded, his eyes pools of terror and pain. 'Robots,' he whispered. 'Or maybe aliens. We saw them. They stood in the middle of the road. The leading Humvee drove straight into one and it was like he had hit a giant redwood. Must have been a robot. Then they attacked. We shot them. Repeatedly, but they didn't even notice. Then the one picked up this truck and threw it at me. Aliens. Help. Mommy?'

The medic inserted a drip and strapped the arm to the torso. But as he did so he looked at the sergeant and shook his head. 'Sorry, gunney, he's gone.'

'Poor kid,' said the sergeant. 'Hallucinating. Fucking robots and aliens and men picking up trucks after they've been shot.'

The sound of an approaching helicopter caused the Seals to look up. A V-22 Osprey tilt rotor transport plane thundered into view. A hybrid cross between a standard airplane and a twin rotor helicopter. Its rotors tilted, and it landed vertically, next to the road.

As it touched down the ramp thumped open and a team of black clad soldiers ran out, assuming a ring of protection around the aircraft.

'Fucking black ops,' muttered the sergeant. 'Here to take over.'

There was a pause, then a man in a black suit, aviator sunglasses, and black Oxfords alighted via the rear ramp. He glanced around then walked straight over to the sergeant.

'Gunnery Sergeant Thomas?'

'Yes, sir,' answered the Navy Seal.

'Thank you for securing the area. You and your men must leave now. And I remind you this never happened. You were never here. Understood?'

'Yes, sir,' acknowledged the sergeant. 'Never happened, sir. Do you need my report, sir?'

The man in the suit shook his head. 'Not necessary, Gunnery Sergeant. Now leave.'

The sergeant circled his hand above his head and the Seal team formed up and double timed it to their Blackhawk helicopter.

They entered and strapped themselves in. Minutes later, the pilot had conducted his preflight and the machine took off, its rotors churning up a cloud of dust and dry grass.

As the Blackhawk levelled out, two men stepped out of the back of the Osprey. Each one carried a MANPAD, man portable aircraft defense missile on their shoulders. They both aimed and fired in seconds, as the helicopter was so close.

The Stinger B missiles struck the helicopter amidships and simply blew it apart in a ball of superheated flame. The area was showered with burning debris, but none of it larger than a grown man's hand.

Seal team seven no longer existed. They had never been there. It had never happened.

The man in the suit beckoned to one of the men in black.

'Yes, colonel?'

'Bag and tag this area,' said the man in the suit. 'Then burn everything. I want no usable evidence left.'

The soldier saluted.

And the man in the suit reached into his jacket pocket, pulled out a travel-sized pump of sanitizing lotion and started to work it into his hands.

He did it three times before he went back to the Osprey.

CHAPTER 20

Brenner pulled the knife from his shoulder and poured some of the alcohol over the wound with a grimace. Then he leaned forward and refilled Solomon's glass.

The man in black raised his glass in a toast. 'Good fight.'

Brenner shrugged. 'Got a bit close at the end.'

'Yep,' agreed Solomon. 'Any reason you didn't just go wolf and end it?'

Brenner lit a cigarette. He didn't offer. 'Can't do that anymore.'

Solomon looked visibly shocked. 'What do you mean? You're no longer a shifter?'

Brenner took a deep drag, then he ripped the arm off his shirt and inspected his knife wound. It had almost halfway healed. If he had been in Wolfman mode, then it would have healed up almost instantly.

'Oh, I'm still a shifter. But if I go wolf

then I can't control myself. Could end up taking out the whole town. Or worse.'

'Since when?'

'Since you jabbed me with that stupid serum of yours. You SOB, you ruined my life.'

Solomon grinned. 'Yeah, sure. I suppose you'd rather be dead? I'm not the bad man here, Brenner,' he continued. 'I saved your life. I'm a fucking Samaritan.'

'You're an asshole,' responded Brenner.

'Unappreciated, unreciprocated, and ignored am I, but I spread the love anyway,' said Solomon in a pious voice. 'Remember, Ded, we rise by lifting others up.'

Brenner growled, and the wolf flashed in his eyes. 'Well then, Samaritan,' he said. 'What are you doing here? Because if you think I'm coming with you then you got another think coming. You try to take me, and I'll go wolf, regardless of the far-reaching consequences, so you and that lackey of yours had better institute a tactical withdrawal before things escalate beyond my control.'

Solomon held his hands up in a conciliatory gesture. 'No,' he said. 'Not here to take you home. Actually, I'm here to ask you for a favor.'

'No,' said Brenner.

'You haven't even heard what it is.'

'Doesn't matter. If it has anything to do with the Bloodborn Project then I want nothing to do with it,' said Brenner.

'Please, Brenner,' urged Solomon. 'Give me five minutes. That's all. After that, if you want me to leave, I'll leave. Deal?'

Brenner grunted, and Solomon took his non-rejection as affirmation.

He told Brenner the story, leaving nothing out.

'Man, that is fucked up,' said Brenner. He lit another cigarette and swigged some more rum. 'And you still think you're the good guys?'

Solomon didn't respond.

'Your precious colonel basically kidnapped a bunch of people and experimented on them without their consent. Killed most of them and ended up creating the mother of all fuck ups that, due to his incompetence, have now been unleashed on an unsuspecting world.'

Still, the man in black said nothing.

'And now you want me, another unwitting victim of your evil, morally corrupt organization, to pull you all out of the shit. You are unbelievable.'

'It's not for us,' said Solomon. 'It's to save innocent people. Brenner, these *Hyaenidae* are feral. They were bad people before the change and now, well let's just say, they have the morality of a pack of hyenas. Enough said.'

'What's in it for me?' asked the big man. 'If I do this can you guarantee the Project will stop looking for me?'

Solomon thought for a few seconds before he shook his head. 'I'm not going to insult you by lying. I could say I could do that, but I very much doubt the colonel would stick to the deal. He's got a real hard on for you and I don't reckon it's ever going to go away.'

'Thanks for being honest,' said Brenner.

'Tell you what,' continued Solomon. 'I'll help you sort out whatever shit you're involved in now, then you give me a hand to subdue these renegade dog boys. One hand washing the other type of deal. Plus, you'll be doing the right thing.'

Brenner sighed. 'I'll help. But only

because someone has to stop them before they start to kill innocent people.'

'Excellent,' approved Solomon. 'And what about your current problem?'

'Drug dealer called Big Yu. Uses the bikers to distribute his drugs across the border into the US. I've taken out most of the bikers, now I've gotta see to Big Yu and whoever else he still has. He lives on a spread out of town.'

'Don't tell me,' interrupted Solomon. 'And your plan was to ride out there tonight, break into the place, kill them all and burn it to the ground?'

Brenner raised an eyebrow. 'Pretty much, yeah. How'd you know?'

Solomon chuckled. 'Ded, my good man,' he answered. 'You are not the subtlest of tacticians. It's all *Veni, vidi, asinus calce.* I came, I saw, I kicked ass.'

The big man shrugged. 'Hey, it works.'

'What's the timing on your masterplan?' asked Solomon.

Brenner took a final swig of rum and slammed the bottle down on the countertop. 'No time like the present,' he answered, as he stood and headed for the door.

CHAPTER 21

The colonel had sent his best men. Fifty of them. Enough to take a small country. Some of the men were armed with MK 48 x 7.62mm machine guns loaded with specially made, depleted uranium armor piercing rounds, and the rest carried the Super Six, semiauto grenade launcher. The colonel was hoping this high level of ordnance would be capable of taking down a *Hyaenidae*.

The black ops team had been inserted at dead of night, via helicopter some two miles away from the Sons HQ town and had traveled from the insertion point on foot so as to avoid detection.

Once they reached their destination, they donned their night vision goggles and split into three groups. The main group of thirty operatives were going to attack the gates. The other two groups of ten were going to flank the town and ingress at the same time. Their instructions were simple.

Kill everyone and everything.

Watches were synchronized, last minute weapons checks carried out and, at precisely seven minutes past midnight, the attack was launched.

The guard towers, and the sentries in them, were taken out by concentrated firepower, both 7.62 rounds and grenades literally disintegrating the structures. Then the grenade launchers tore holes in the gate and fences alike.

The special operatives poured through the breaches and spread out, working from building to building.

But apart from the single guards on the four towers, there seemed to be no more resistance.

Captain Thomson from the main group, radioed through to sergeant Clark. 'Sergeant, see any opposition?'

'Negative, Captain. All quiet.'

'Sergeant Bulmer? Resistance?' questioned the captain as he contacted the third group.

'Deadsville, Captain. Some lights are on, and I think that I can hear music, but no sign of any tangos yet.'

'Continue searching,' commanded the

captain. 'Keep your eyes peeled and stay frosty, I don't like this.'

The fifty operatives ghosted through the town, peering into windows, and around corners, keeping low. Keeping silent.

Captain Thomson crept around a corner and moved slowly down an alleyway between two buildings close to the center of the town. Halfway down the alley he glanced down and left to see a small red light on the wall of one of the buildings. He looked to his right and picked out a small mirror. He had just walked through an infrared beam of some sort.

His stomach fell as he realized what was happening. Bringing the radio to his lips he keyed the open channel. 'Run,' he shouted. 'Get the fuck out of here. Move.'

But it was too late.

The M18A Claymore contains approximately twenty-four ounces of C4 explosive and seven hundred steel balls that explode out to a lethal distance of around fifty-five yards.

Anubis had gotten his troops to lay sixty-two mines in various positions around the town. A combined total of almost one hundred pounds of C4 propelling over forty thousand steel balls. These were all connected to an infrared trip beam near the center of the town to ensure that the attackers would have instituted a full ingress.

This detonation was also connected to approximately two tons of ammonium nitrate based "fertilizer bombs" that were strapped to over one hundred, forty-four-gallon drums of aviation fuel.

The resulting explosion was seen as far away as Huntsville and Chattanooga. Almost a hundred miles.

The Sons had struck their first blow.

***

Over three hundred miles away, Anubis stood on the roof of the cab of a two-ton truck and surveyed the new camp. The entirety of The Sons had moved to an abandoned gold mine near Cave City, Kentucky, leaving four brave volunteers at Battelle to strike the first blow against the left.

To be fair, the volunteers were all family men who were actually given little choice. Volunteer for the good of the movement, or your entire extended family dies a terrible death.

True patriots. They would be remembered.

And now it was time to escalate the cause.

CHAPTER 22

'Let's simply unload a whole bunch of ordnance at the place, pour a few gallons of gas over the rubble, torch it and move on,' said Solomon. 'Howard here can take care of anyone who tries to escape. Should take us all of ten minutes.'

Brenner shook his head. 'What if there are innocents inside?'

'Collateral damage, old sport,' argued the man in black. 'Omelets, eggs, and that sort of thing. We knock this little problem on the head then go and do some real work, what do you say?'

'I say that this is real work,' answered Brenner. 'This dude is bringing drugs into the US. Bad drugs. Not talking a bit of dope for potheads, we're talking Fentanyl. It makes heroin look like cotton candy. So, we hit this place hard, we take out all that deserve to be taken out, then we split. But first we check. Collateral damage is unacceptable.'

'And who decides who deserves to be taken out?' asked Howard.

Brenner turned his gaze to the driver-come-hitman with distaste. 'I do,' he said. 'And you don't talk to me. Ever. Or you won't talk again. You hear?'

Howard looked like he was about to answer when Solomon caught his eye and shook his head slightly. Brenner didn't make idle threats. He didn't even entertain them as a concept. And Solomon didn't particularly enjoy driving so he wanted to keep his assistant alive.

'Fine,' said the man in black. 'I'll go in and do a recce. Wait here.'

'No,' argued Brenner. 'I'll go.'

'Listen, big man,' said Solomon. 'I got full respect for your stealth capabilities when you're in wolf mode, but if you are going to insist on staying human, then let uncle Solomon do the sneaky stuff. OK? Trust me, you can't compete.'

Brenner saw the sense in what Solomon was saying, so with a curt nod, he acquiesced.

Solomon headed towards the fence surrounding the house and environs and, as they watched him, he simply disappeared into the night.

Twenty minutes later he reappeared some ten yards away and hurried over.

'Right,' he said. 'Big place. Loads of guards. They must have heard of the incident at the bar because everyone is awake and tooled up. Maybe twenty-four guards outside. Can't tell inside. At least another ten. Thought I could hear female voices, or at least one female voice. But not talking. Crying maybe. They sounded in distress. Not in any room with an outside wall or window. As far as I could tell, no tripwires, no infrared, no dogs. Managed to take a look into the kitchen; no cooks or servants. Everyone I did see was carrying so, all fair game.'

'So, a pretty simple smash and destroy,' added Brenner.

Solomon nodded. 'Howard. You take a position on the hill there. Provide overwatch. Take the long gun and some of the heavy stuff. One can never have too much ordnance. Take your cues from us, kill anyone who tries to escape.'

The man in black opened the trunk of the BMW, hauled out a weapon and bandolier, and handed it to Brenner. 'Take this. If you aren't going to use your skills, then you'll need extra firepower. This should suit your gung ho, bull-in-a-china-shop methods.'

Brenner gave the weapon a quick once over. It was an AA-12 fully automatic shotgun. Loaded with a thirty-two-round drum magazine of twelve gauge double aught. The bandolier held another three drums. Over one hundred and twenty rounds of bad intentions ready to rock and roll.

The big man grinned. 'Let's do it.'

While Howard went to his overwatch position, Brenner and Solomon headed for the perimeter fence. Solomon led Brenner to a dark area at the rear of the compound. They checked for sentries, found none, then simply jumped over the ten-foot-high chain-link fence. Because, even in human mode, Brenner was still vastly superior to any Olympic athlete in their prime.

Together they ghosted towards the main house. Two guards came around the corner of one of the outbuildings but, even though both Brenner and Solomon were almost on top of them, they didn't see them until it was too late. Brenner grabbed the one guard, wrapped his arm around his neck and jerked, snapping it like a chopstick. Solomon went the bloodier route and used his talons to remove the guards head. Blood sprayed over the two of them and Brenner grimaced.

'Really?' he asked. 'You gotta paint us all with gore? What the fuck, dude.'

Solomon grinned. 'Welcome to the suck, big man.'

Brenner shook his head. 'Nutcase,' he grunted.

The next two guards went the same way.

The third set that they came across, consisted of three instead if two. Brenner took out the one while Solomon decapitated one then eviscerated the next, literally tearing his guts out, clamping a hand over his mouth to silence him as he died.

'Ah, variety,' he said with a grin. 'The spice of life.'

'You need therapy, dude,' said Brenner. 'Seriously.'

'This is my therapy,' quipped the gore-spattered man in black.

They managed to exterminate six more

guards before they ran into a slight glitch. Brenner took his out while Solomon did the same, but as they were doing so, a further couple of guards walked around a corner and saw them.

Both Brenner and Solomon leapt onto their prey, but as they did so, the one sentry pressed a panic button that was hanging on a necklace around his neck. There was a loud blaring of an alarm and, at the same time, thick steel shutters came crashing down over all ingress points to the house.

Simultaneously, a raft of floodlights slammed on, bathing the entire area in a white, electric glare.

Solomon put his hands on his hips. 'Well, that is sure to spice things up.'

Groups of armed guards came rushing at them from all sides, snapping off rounds as they came.

Brenner hauled up his AA-12 and pulled the trigger, spewing out double aught rounds at a rate of five per second. Seven seconds later, nine guards lay dead or dying.

'I think that's all of them,' said Solomon.

Brenner nodded at the steel-clad building in front of them. 'We seem to have developed a slight access problem. Any suggestions?'

Solomon smirked. 'Sure. Allow me.' He took out a small two-way radio and thumbed the call button. 'Howard, be so good as to provide us with an access point. Main door if you would.'

There was a sharp crack, followed by a whooshing sound then, in a blinding flash of light, a massive explosion that tore a hole through the steel shuttered front door. The shock wave pushed Brenner backwards, almost knocking him off his feet.

'M47 Dragon anti-tank missile,' said Solomon. 'Perfect for those nights when you've lost your keys.' He bowed and gestured towards the breach. 'After you, old sport.'

Brenner took point and the two of them ran into the building.

The house was a sprawling bungalow that seemed to have had various extensions and additions added on in random fashion. Rooms adjoined each other with no interleading corridors, two doors would open into the same room, some rooms were entirely internal with no windows or access to natural light. Hive mentality as opposed to architectural logic.

Armed guards popped up like plates in a shooting gallery, banging off a couple of rounds then ducking down again.

Brenner took them out using overwhelming force. Every guard got a two second burst of buckshot. Ten rounds. It was immaterial whether they ducked behind a sofa, or a door, or a bed, the end result was the same. Whatever they took cover behind got shredded, then they did too.

It didn't take long, and the house was cleared. Except for one central room. It was protected by a single steel-clad door. Above the door was a small CCTV camera. The big man and Solomon stood outside the door and contemplated it.

'Go wolf and knock it down,' suggested the man in black.

Brenner shook his head.

'Well what then?' asked Solomon. 'I can't get Howard to launch a missile at it, it's impossible.'

Brenner replaced the drum magazine to

his shotgun, placed the end of the barrel against the hinge side of the door at the top and pulled the trigger. As the weapon hammered out its five rounds a second, Brenner dragged the weapon down the side of the door, like he was drawing a line. By the time he got to the bottom of the doorframe, a splintered crack ran from top to bottom. He swung the shotgun behind him, letting it rest on its sling, took two steps back then launched himself forward.

The door smashed off its weakened hinges like hurricane Katrina had entered the building.

'Avon calling,' announced Solomon as the two of them stormed into the room.

Three Vietnamese men stood together at the far side of the room. All were heavily armed. A fourth sat behind a large, ornately carved desk, his hands steepled in front of him. An expression of quiet contemplation on his face.

The armed men opened up. Bullets buzzed and spat around both Solomon and Brenner. One round clipped the big man's shoulder in a puff of blood, but it didn't even cause him to flinch. Not one shot got anywhere close to Solomon as he attacked with eye-confounding speed.

Blood sprayed high. The sound of flesh being torn and bones breaking filled the room.

Then three men lay still on the floor, throats torn open, arms smashed, fingers missing, and faces covered in deep gashes.

Brenner had to admit to himself that he was impressed. Sometimes he forgot how fast Solomon could move when he put his mind to it.

The man in black stood above the vanquished men and shook his head. 'Vietnamese,' he said. 'Man, talk about having flashbacks.'

Brenner walked up to the man behind the desk and stared at him. 'Big Yu?'

The man nodded. 'Yes. However, you have the advantage over me. Who are you?'

'I'm the dude that stops people like you. I am retribution.'

Big Yu nodded. His face an almost inscrutable mask. Almost, because lurking there, was a glimmer of fear that he could not hide. 'You were there,' he said.

'Where?' asked Brenner.

'The war. You were there,' repeated Big

Yu.

'How could I have been?' asked Brenner. 'I'm too young.'

The drug dealer shook huis head. 'No, you were there. It's in the eyes. I can see it. As plain as a facial tattoo.'

Brenner nodded. 'We were both there,' he confirmed.

'We won,' stated Big Yu. 'We beat the mighty war machine of the USA. You lost.'

'Yes,' admitted Brenner. 'But this time, we won.' Then he tilted his head to one side and sniffed the air, his human senses still attuned to the wolf in him, even though he had not changed. Without saying anything he prowled around the room, stopping in front of a large oil painting of Ho Chi Minh. The big man grabbed the frame and ripped the painting off the wall to reveal a concealed doorway.

He tried the handle to find it wasn't locked, so he opened the door and walked in. A small landing area led to a steep flight of steps. He went down them, weapon ready. At the bottom, a good-sized concrete basement. A naked bulb provided barely enough light to see. The floor was bare concrete, as were the walls and ceiling.

But the first thing that hit Brenner was the smell. Blood and sweat and fear.

Glancing around him, Brenner saw a light switch and he flicked it. A series of bulbs flickered on, filling the room with a harsh electric glare. In the far corner, Brenner heard someone whimper.

He walked over to see a cage. Maybe six feet by six by six. It had been fabricated from thick bamboo and lashed together with wire. Simple, crude, and effective. Brenner had seen similar, during his time in Vietnam. American prisoners kept in rows of them. Starving, tortured, and broken.

He approached the cage to see that there was single occupant.

And rage washed over him like a tsunami.

A young girl. Semi-naked, threadbare underwear. Dark hair, cut short and ragged. Dirty but not filthy. But the worst of it was the network of shallow cuts that crisscrossed her entire body like a tattoo of chain link fencing. Some were fresh, some older and healed.

Brenner approached the cage slowly, his hands held in front of him. Then he stopped and squatted down a couple of yards away.

'Hey,' he said, his voice low and gentle. 'I'm not going to hurt you. The dudes upstairs have been taken care of. I'm going to open the cage now, OK? Please do not worry or be scared. I am your friend.'

He shuffled forward, grasped the padlock, and simply twisted it off with a burst of strength.

The door swung open, but the girl didn't move.

'Come on, sweetheart,' said Brenner. 'Let's get you out of here, go someplace safe and nice. Get some food and drink and a clean bed.'

Slowly, eyes cast down, body clenched in fear, the girl started to move. As she approached the door and came more into the light, Brenner could see that his initial impression of her had been incorrect. She wasn't a young girl. She was a woman. Probably in her early to mid-twenties. Full figured, and muscular at the same time. But small. Maybe five two or three.

As she stepped out of the cage, Brenner

took off his leather coat and draped it over her. It was large enough on her petite frame to almost touch the floor, like a medieval cloak.

The big man led the girl up the stairs and out into the study above.

'What's this?' asked Solomon.

Brenner shook his head. 'No idea. There were a bunch of bamboo cages. She was in one of them. You remember those cages from 'Nam? Obviously, his private torture project.'

Solomon nodded, and his eyes glinted with dark fury as memories best left buried rose to the fore.

'So, what now?' continued the man in black.

Brenner stared at the Vietnamese drug lord. 'What you are disgusts me,' he said. 'Not only the drugs but this,' he pointed at the girl. 'Whatever this is. You are a craven excuse for a human being, and as such, you forfeit the right to be treated with any respect or dignity.' The big man turned to Solomon. 'I'm going to take the girl outside. Could you do me a favor?'

Solomon nodded.

'Kill this thing. Take your time. Make

sure that he dies, understanding the depth of his sin.'

The man in black nodded again. Then he smiled, his exaggerated canines glistening in the overhead lights.

Brenner led the girl outside. They went and stood by the gates. The big man lit a cigarette and offered it. She shook her head. A minute later, Howard appeared, driving the BMW.

In the distance, but still clearly audible, they could hear Big Yu screaming in agony absolute. After ten minutes the screaming dwindled to a whimper. Then a gurgle.

Then silence.

Solomon walked out of the building and approached, his forearms glistened with fresh blood.

'It's done,' he said to Brenner.

'Thanks.'

Then Solomon turned to Howard. 'Take some thermite grenades,' he commanded. 'Go inside and spread them around. I want this place burned to the ground.'

They stood together in silence until Howard returned and, with a thumping explosion, the building started to burn.

'Let's blow this town,' said Solomon. 'Head out, find a decent hotel and get some clothes for the girl. We can plan our next move after that.'

Brenner guided the girl to the BMW, but she shook her head and pulled away.

'Come on, sweetheart,' he said. 'We gotta get going.'

Again, she shook her head. Then she pointed at the Harley.

'No way,' said Brenner. 'You can't ride with me. Go in the car. It's safer and more comfortable.'

But the girl ignored him and, instead, walked over to the rat bike, climbed onto the saddle, and waited.

Brenner sighed. 'Fine,' he said. 'Just hold tight, OK?'

She nodded.

Solomon grinned at the big man's discomfort and got into the limousine.

Howard pulled off and Brenner followed, trusting in Solomon's choice of destination.

CHAPTER 23

Solomon had booked them into the Grand hotel, Great Falls, Montana. They had arrived just before daybreak and, although the place was way above the class of hotel Brenner normally frequented, he didn't have the energy to argue.

The man in black had booked four separate rooms but the girl had followed Brenner to his room and simply refused to leave, shaking her head whenever he tried to get her to.

They had no idea what her name was or even where she was from, as since they had rescued her, she still hadn't uttered a word. Brenner had tried to question her, but although she listened to him and acknowledged his questions with either a raised eyebrow or slight nod, she didn't answer or converse in any way whatsoever. Silent. Mute.

Brenner had ordered room service breakfast for the two of them, eggs, bacon, link sausages, toast, and fresh orange juice. She had eaten ravenously, pausing occasionally to breathe deeply then continue.

Solomon had tasked his assistant with getting the girl some clothes and, after breakfast, Howard knocked on the door and Brenner let him in. The driver simply handed Brenner a small rucksack and left without comment.

The big man closed the door and gave the girl the rucksack. She peered inside, stood from her chair, and went through to the bathroom.

The shower turned on and stayed on for almost an hour. After the water stopped, another half an hour passed. Then the bathroom door opened, and, with a billow of steam, the girl revealed herself.

Howard had done a perfect job of sizing her. And for some reason he had decided she should be dressed in exactly the same fashion as Brenner. Well fitted jeans, a tight white t-shirt, leather belt, leather jacket and military style boots.

He had also purchased makeup, and the girl had applied it liberally, but well.

Purple eyeshadow, swept up from her

eyes, thick black eyeliner, mascara, and lip gloss as red as desire and as shiny as lust. Her chopped black hair stood in spikes. A Visigoth war bonnet.

She looked at Brenner and he could swear she growled. Low and quiet. Almost a purr.

'Wow,' he said. 'You look … better. How do you feel?'

She shrugged and went back to the breakfast table to finish off any of the remaining scraps.

'I can order more, if you want,' said Brenner.

She looked up at him then nodded.

The big man picked up the phone and ordered the same again.

An hour later, she had finished the next tranche of food and leaned back in the chair, a look of satisfaction on her face.

There was a knock on the door and Solomon walked in without invitation. 'I've just had news from the colonel,' he said.

'What's the son of a bitch have to say?' asked Brenner.

'He sent a team to the dog boys HQ. A ghost town called Battelle, in Alabama.

Fifty black ops specialists. But they were set up. Walked into an ambush. The Sons weren't there. Well, they left a token guard, enough to look like the place was still operative, then when the team infiltrated, the whole town was wired to blow. Place went up like Krakatoa. Killed every one of them. He sent a follow up team of techie types. They found four enemy bodies, fifty of our boys. No sign or clue of the rest of the movement.'

'There's always a sign,' said Brenner 'You just need to look hard enough, question enough people.'

'Reckon we should go take a look ourselves?'

The big man nodded. 'It's the only lead we got.'

'I concur,' said Solomon. 'We'll spend the night here, get some sleep, then tomorrow, we move out.'

CHAPTER 24

'And so begins the next phase of our war,' said Anubis. 'From this day on, the sons shall begin their campaign. First, we gather funding, while at the same time spreading the word. Telling the world of our presence. Warning the communists and Jews of our coming. Striking fear into the hearts of the left, the godless and the weak.'

The Sons stamped their feet and cheered, screaming out their version of the rebel yell. 'Hoowee! Hoowee!'

Behind Anubis, the permanents raised their muzzles and howled in concert, a guttural, jabbering, insane laugh.

'Two groups will go forth,' continued the Alpha. 'Under the leadership of Osiris and Set. Eight males, two female stormtroopers and one permanent in each group. These forces will be tasked with the collection of funds gained by confiscating money from the Jewish run banks. At the same time, we shall leave our mark, showing that a new movement has started. The new flag of the Fatherland will be left flying at each bank we call on. Long live the Sons of One Eight.'

'Long live Anubis,' cheered the crowd. 'Long live the Sons.'

When the cheering had died down, Anubis called his two officers to him and explained their mission in more depth.

Team, Osiris would go east, to Dayton in Pennsylvania. There they would strike the Dayton Family Bank, taking all they could, destroying the place, and raising the flag outside.

Team Set were to go west. Coldwater, Kansas. Their mission parameters were the same. Collateral damage was encouraged, as any person banking with a Jewish establishment was considered fair game.

Each team, was to be supplied with a Ford transit passenger wagon, capable of carrying fifteen people, as well as sufficient weapons and supplies. However, Anubis made it plain; he wanted the bulk of the intimidation and destruction to be done by the clan members. The *Hyaenidae,* both *sapiens* and permanents.

'The people must see,' he said. 'They must know of the unstoppable power they face. They must be made fully aware of the superiority of the new master race.'

After the first hit, team Osiris would then continue on to Illinois, and team Set to Minnesota. There they would strike another two banks. Hitting hard and fast, maximum damage. Theater.

'Drive through the night,' urged Anubis. 'There will be time for rest later. We must give the impression we are larger in numbers than we are, and this operation will be the start. Go, my children. Go forth and sow the seeds of a new nation.'

***

Howard parked the BMW a few yards from the destroyed gates of the ghost town. Brenner pulled in behind him, the girl riding pillion.

The sun was still up, so the big man did the recce with the girl whilst Solomon sheltered in the car avoiding the sunlight.

It didn't take the pair long to deduce the fact there was little to go on. The entire town had been eradicated. The combination of C4 and fertilizer bombs had flattened the buildings and left massive craters in their place. Afterwards, Brenner did a few slow circuits of the town, spreading his search out in an expanding spiral pattern. On his fifth circumference he came across what he was searching for. A staging area in the woods.

It had been well cleaned and backtracked, but the perpetrators had not counted on Brenner's wolflike sense of smell. He followed the tracks for half an hour, pausing occasionally to check the girl was still with him.

After he had ensured the direction was true, he turned back, beckoning to the girl to continue to follow him. By the time they returned to the BMW, the sun was going down and Solomon was standing outside, leaning against the door.

'So, he said. 'You're back. And I see Shadow is still with you.'

'Shadow?'

Solomon nodded. 'She needs a name. Can't keep calling her, girl. And I reckoned she's as close as you get to being your shadow, so, that's her name.'

'Fair enough,' conceded Brenner. 'As

far as I can tell, they went north. But when they exit the forest they split up. It's almost impossible to tell where they were heading.'

Solomon nodded. 'It's something. I'll get hold of my guys, tell them to point their sights north of here, get the FBI to question the local police, law enforcement, private contractors. Also, we'll see if we can get some eye's-in-the-sky. Look for any convoys, heavy vehicles. Anything suspicious.'

'You can do all that?' sked Brenner.

The man in black nodded.

'Well how come you never use it to find me?'

Solomon shook his head. 'We do. But America's a huge place and you're just one man. And a man who's good at keeping a low profile. Most of the time, that is. Hard to find such a small needle in such a large haystack.'

'Well do it, then,' said Brenner, as he mounted his bike. 'And meanwhile, let's head north.'

CHAPTER 25

Rocky Norman was forty-two years old and fitter than your average twenty-year-old. He had done two tours of Iraq, one in Afghanistan and six years in Europe. Now he was retired but, as they say, once a Marine, always a Marine. He had a license for concealed carry, and he packed a Colt .45 with a Para-Ordnance frame and compensator. This meant he had thirteen rounds in his weapon instead of the usual seven. He also reloaded his own ammo, so his rounds were hot and heavy. Maybe fifty percent harder hitting than store bought.

He stood in the short queue behind an old lady with a flowered hat and a middle-aged man who looked like the quintessential accountant. It was a Friday afternoon and, as such, a few of the people in the bank were drawing wages for their farmhands, workers, and weekly expenses.

And Rocky wasn't the only one who

was armed.

It took the clients a while to realize the bank was actually being robbed. This was because the two men who walked inside were not armed. In fact, they both looked slightly crippled. Both had hunched backs. The politically correct term was kyphosis, but in rural Kansas, people assumed that was something Superman was allergic to.

And the one robber who wore a deep cowl over his head, seemed to have something wrong with his legs. Almost like he was wearing blades under his trousers. They looked like the joints were bending backwards, like a dog.

So, when the unarmed leader jumped up onto one of the customer desks and informed everyone they should lie down on the floor and remain silent as a robbery was taking place, he was met with an equal amount of both incredulity and amusement.

The security guard didn't even bother to draw his weapon, he simply shook his head and told the man to leave.

'Listen, boy,' he instructed. 'A joke's a joke, but we can't have you coming in here and jumping on the furniture, you might hurt yourself or break something. So why don't you come on down then you and you friend can leave. Quickly now, sonny, before I get angry.'

Rocky and a couple of other people in the queue chuckled softly. *The youth of today*, seemed to be the general consensus.

However, the hunchbacked man remained standing on the desk and repeated his instructions.

With a snort of irritation, the security guard strode over and grabbed the man's leg. 'Come on, sonny,' he said. 'Get down now.'

The crippled man leaned down, grabbed the guards right arm and, with a violent twist, literally tore it off.

A spray of blood arced across the room and the guard fell to the floor screaming in agony.

Then the man on the table threw his head back and howled. A sharp, demented sound. A combination of insane laughter and primal savagery.

At the same time, his cry was joined by the man with the hood and the oddly shaped legs. A yipping, evil laugh that brought shivers to Rocky's flesh and sent fear crackling through his brain.

But Rocky had seen lots of action before. He had seen men killed and he had killed in return. He was no small-town security guard, or middle management accountant. He was the product of one of the greatest fighting forces in the world. And he didn't take no shit from a couple of freaks.

Drawing his Colt, he lined it up with the man on the desk and yelled out. 'Hey, asshole. Get some.'

He pulled the trigger six times. Every round struck the perpetrator center mass. Flawless shooting.

Then Rocky swiveled and drew a bead on the second perp, shouting a warning before he fired. 'Down on the floor, asshat,' he shouted. 'Do it now, or I fire.'

The perp ignored Rocky's command entirely and started to walk towards him.

Again, Rocky's weapon barked. This time he used the Mozambique drill, also known as the Failure to Stop drill. A double tap to center mass and then a follow up shot to the head.

The Marine executed it perfectly.

The first two shots had no effect

whatsoever. The third shot struck the man in the face and ripped his hood back.

And Rocky realized what he was shooting at wasn't human. The creature opposite him growled, exposing three-inch canines, a large, feral muzzle, and bloodshot yellow eyes. Out of the corner of his vision, Rocky noticed the first man he had shot was also totally unaffected and was simply standing easy and watching.

Then, with a grin, the leader gestured towards Rocky and gave the command. 'Finish him.'

The Marine managed to get off his last four shots before the creature grabbed him and threw him across the room like a small child, smashing his head into the wall with a meaty thud.

Then the real killing started.

Two minutes later, Osiris opened the bank doors and let the stormtroopers in. He had already torn the door off the vault and now it was up to the troops to clean the bank out.

Another ten minutes and they were leaving.

A single sheriff's car tried to intercept them on the way out, but a blast of automatic fire shredded the vehicle, killing all inside and putting a swift end to any pursuit.

Then they headed for Illinois.

CHAPTER 26

Team Set's first operation did not go as smoothly as team Osiris'. They hit the bank in the same way, Set and the permanent going in first. The guard was terminally subdued, and the vault torn open. However, due to the unforeseen fact that there was a local symposium of private security companies being held at the Holiday Inn a block away, the response to the silent alarm was totally out of proportion to what was expected.

Fully twenty vehicles filled to the brim with weekend warriors, local police, and out of town private security guards arrived, like the 5th cavalry coming to the rescue.

As per instructions, the stormtroopers outside the bank opened fire on the security forces. Cars exploded, and windows shattered as thousands of rounds buzzed and shrieked through the air. The Stormtroopers were hopelessly outnumbered but, on the plus side, they had superior fire power. And once their two SAW machine guns added their voices to the fray, the engagement settled into a Mexican standoff. Both sides entrenched behind cover and firing the odd shot at each other.

Then Set and the permanent emerged from the bank.

Set had morphed into his full Hyena mode. The size of a pony, head larger than a male child's torso, and teeth that defied description. Canines a hand's breadth wide and over six inches long, from which thick ropes of saliva dangled.

And his jabbering howl rent the air like a thousand maniacs vocalizing their insane anger at the same time.

After a few seconds of shocked silence, the entire collection of security guards and police opened up on the two creatures. The volume of firepower was overwhelming, and both Set and the permanent staggered back as they absorbed the punishment. But the pause in their forward momentum was fleeting as they simply pushed back, shrugging off the barrage of bullets as they attacked.

Vehicles were thrown out of the way,

and shooters were dispatched with extreme prejudice. Limbs torn from sockets, craniums shattered by massive jaws, backs broken by being tossed across the road into concrete walls.

Very few guards stood their ground as the inhuman fury descended on them.

And all the while, the stormtroopers added their firepower.

Mere minutes later, the street was strewn with bodies, both dead and dying. Set morphed back into human mode and shouted instructions.

'Get inside. Fill the money bags and let's move out.'

Shortly afterward, team Set left Coldwater, Kansas and headed for Minnesota. They had lost two stormtroopers and one was wounded.

Acceptable losses.

***

A pair of V-22 Osprey tilt rotor transport planes thundered into the airspace above Dayton, Pennsylvania. Then, with a deftness that belied the huge size of the aircraft, they settled down in the street opposite the bank.

The rear ramps deployed and disgorged forty-eight, black clad, special operations troops. With their faces hidden behind cotton masks and goggles. Fully kitted out in Kevlar helmets and vests and ultra-modern tactical equipment, they looked almost as alien as the *Hyaenidae* had.

They quickly formed a perimeter around the area, cordoning off streets and shutting down access to buildings and clearing everyone from the immediate vicinity.

Finally, when the area was totally locked down, the colonel deplaned.

The senior black ops officer ran over to him and informed him the area was secure as instructed.

'The entire vicinity has been cordoned off, sir,' said the operative. 'We have two survivors. An old lady and a middle-aged man. I think the man has done service. Most likely Marines.'

'Take me to them,' instructed the colonel.

The operative led his CO to the bank. The two survivors were lying on the floor. They both had drips inserted and were covered by shiny silver space blankets. Their heads propped up on thin pillows.

The colonel approached the Marine first, going down on one knee next to him. 'So, you survived,' he said. 'You have the look of someone who has served.'

The Marine nodded. 'PFC. Marine Corps, colonel. Oorah,' he answered. 'And it'll take more than those SOB's have got to take out one of Uncle Sam's finest.' He coughed painfully.

The colonel patted the man on his shoulder and smiled. 'Oorah, PFC. Now, tell me, what happened here?'

The Marine shook his head. 'It's gonna sound crazy, sir,' he said, his voice rough with pain. 'But I think that we were attacked by ... I'm not actually sure, sir. Aliens? Whatever, they certainly weren't human. Although the one looked human. The other, though ... some sort of animal thing. I put six shots into the one, and seven into the other. They just laughed at me, sir. Like shooting at a main battle tank. And fast, like lightning. Also, stronger than a hundred men put together. I swear, sir,' urged the injured Marine. 'Ask anyone else, I'm not making this up.'

'But you survived,' noted the colonel.

'Fucking A, sir,' concurred the Marine. 'I'm still here to tell the tale.'

'Yes,' agreed the colonel. 'Pity.'

'Sorry, sir?'

'I said, it's a pity,' concluded the colonel as he leaned forward and covered the Marine's mouth with his left hand. Using his thumb, he flicked open the blade of his Strider SMF lock blade and plunged it into the wounded man's neck, working it back and forth as he did so.

Rocky Norman shuddered for a few seconds then lay still. There would be no stories of aliens, or super strong animals, or bulletproof assailants. At least not from him.

The colonel stood and went over to kneel beside the old lady.

'Hello, my dear,' he greeted her, his lock blade concealed in his right hand. 'So, you survived. Tell me what you saw.'

CHAPTER 27

Solomon put his cell back in his pocket and frowned. 'That was the colonel,' he said. 'Apparently the dog boys have been busy. Four hits on banks. Kansas, Pennsylvania, Illinois, and Minnesota. All in the last two days. Sounds like they really tore the places up. No regard for collateral damage. No survivors.'

'We're close to Kansas,' replied Brenner. 'What town?'

'A place called Coldwater,' said Solomon.

'Let's go and check it out,' said Brenner. 'See if we can get any leads.'

Solomon shook his head. 'The colonel says not to bother. His guys have already cased the scene. There's nothing to go on. He says better to wait for some more concrete evidence as to where the Sons are hiding out, then we can hit them there.'

'So, he says we can't go and give the place the once over?' asked Brenner.

'Yep,' concurred the man in black. 'We wait for his go ahead.'

'Yeah, well, fuck him,' said Brenner. 'I'm going to Coldwater to do a recce. I don't do sitting on my ass waiting for the bureaucrats to pull their finger out.'

'The colonel won't be pleased,' warned Solomon.

'Well the colonel can kiss my hairy ass,' responded Brenner. 'Are you coming?'

Solomon nodded. 'Might as well. The shit's gonna hit the fan, whatever I do.'

'Good man,' said Brenner. 'Let's pack up and head out ASAP.'

***

Howard had driven Solomon to the Holiday Inn, a block from the bank that got hit. While the two of them booked rooms, Brenner and Shadow went to check out the bank.

There wasn't much to see. The area was still cordoned off with yellow police tape, but Brenner could get close enough to see the bullet marks in the concrete, the broken windows, and the smashed doors. Also, burned out cars and trashed motorbikes littered the street.

It had obviously been a serious firefight. But his wolf's sense of smell told him more. Blood. Lots of it. More than should be present from mere gunshot wounds. Brenner had come across that before. In fact, had been the perpetrator of the same types of violence. The massive amounts of blood were due to combatants having been torn apart. Limb from limb. And over that a subtle feral scent. Wet dog and rotting meat.

There was no mistaking the *Hyaenidae* had been there.

He proceeded to trawl the surrounds, knocking on doors, and asking questions. He didn't need to pretend to be a reporter, or a private eye to get people to talk. Because Brenner had learned long before; people loved to tell what they knew. Even if they knew nothing. And in this case, that was what he was getting. Many people had a story to tell, but the ones who talked knew nothing of substance. They knew the bank had been robbed. There had been lots of shooting. Helicopters or similar had arrived shortly afterwards and … well, that was that.

No actual eye witnesses.

No factual corroboration.

Nothing.

It was almost as if every eye witness had been gotten rid of. As if the area had been sterilized.

After a couple of hours of the same, Brenner knew he was wasting his time, and he and Shadow went to the hotel.

Upon arriving, he saw Solomon had booked him and the girl into the same room, with two single beds. Brenner didn't mind as he knew Shadow would have refused to stay in her own room at any rate.

They unloaded their small amount of luggage then went to call on the man in black.

'It's a cover-up,' stated Brenner without preamble as he entered the room.

'No way,' said Solomon sarcastically. 'You don't say? The establishment are trying to cover up the fact that a clan of human-hyena hybrids have escaped a secret government facility and are robbing banks and waging a war against the democratically voted leadership of the country.'

'Fuck you, Solomon,' responded Brenner. 'I don't just mean a men-in-black, forget-what-you-saw type cover-up. I couldn't find a single person who had eyeballed the happening. Or any part of it.'

'So?' asked the man in black.

'So, it means someone got rid of them,' answered Brenner. 'Like, permanently.'

Solomon shook his head. 'No way. The colonel wouldn't get rid of innocent Americans. He's a patriot. I know you don't like him, but he loves his country.'

'Oh, wake up, Solomon,' shouted Brenner. 'That snake would kill his own mother if he thought she was getting in the way of his ultimate objective.'

The man in black stood. 'The sun's down,' he said. 'Howard and I will go forth and seek out these eye witnesses for you. Trust me, Brenner, they are there, you simply missed them when you were blundering around like some amateur detective. And when I get back with proof, you are going to eat those false accusations.'

Shadow stood and growled softly at Solomon, daring him to make any sort of hostile movement towards Brenner.

But the big man waved her back and shook his head. 'I hope you're correct,' he said. 'Really, I do.'

Solomon stormed out of the room.

'If there are any witnesses out there, he will find them,' said the big man to Shadow. 'He has a knack for finding information. But I don't think there are any, and that fact terrifies him. Because it blemishes all he stands for.'

Shadow walked over and rubbed Brenner's back, purring softly.

'Should I order some food?' asked Brenner.

Shadow smiled and nodded.

CHAPTER 28

Solomon knocked on the door and Brenner let him in. It was four thirty in the morning, but Solomon hadn't woken the big man up as he had been waiting.

Shadow was asleep in her bed, her bedclothes pulled up over her head.

Brenner poured two healthy measures of Jack and handed one to the man in black, saying nothing.

They both sat at the small table in the room.

As it was a smoking room, Brenner lit up a Lucky Strike and waited.

Eventually, Solomon spoke. 'He had them all killed,' he said. His voice dead. Emotionless. 'Men, women. Even children. Some bodies were taken away. Others left in situ. Heart attacks. Falling down the stairs. Two suicides. Nine people including a little girl. She was seven. Nothing overt, but I've seen it all before. Fuck me, I've done it myself.'

He took a sip of his whisky.

'Seven years old,' he repeated.

Still Brenner said nothing. This was not a time for I-told-you. This was a time for quiet reflection and support.

'Nine innocent Americans, and they were the ones I could track down. Maybe even more.' Solomon downed the rest of his drink and poured another. 'So, what have you got to say?'

Brenner shrugged.

'How about, that's what I said. Or, what did you expect?'

'I'm sorry,' said Brenner.

'You and me both,' responded the man in black.

The two of them sat in silence for another ten minutes or so. Then Solomon said. 'The same will have happened at the other raids. Who knows how many will die as this continues? Who knows how big the cover-up will become? We have to stop him.'

'Article 95, section 894,' stated Brenner.

Solomon looked blank for a few seconds then it registered. 'Mutiny or sedition,' he intoned. 'The intent of a person who does usurp or override military authority, refuses, in concert with any other person, to obey orders or otherwise do his duty or creates any violence or disturbance is guilty of mutiny.'

'And a person who is found guilty of attempted mutiny, mutiny, sedition, or failure to suppress or report a mutiny or sedition shall be punished by death,' finished Brenner, quoting the military law verbatim. 'You can't just decide to off your superior officer. Anyway, it would be close to impossible to get to him.'

'Easy,' contradicted Solomon. 'I simply ask for a meeting, as soon as we're alone, I rip his head off.'

'Suicide mission,' said Brenner. 'No, stop and think for a while. The best way to stop this is to stop the *Hyaenidae*. To exterminate the Sons of One Eight. Flush the whole lot of them down the fucking toilet. Then we can talk about your precious colonel.'

Solomon poured another drink then nodded. 'True. So, what next? I've got all my contacts looking but, *nada*.'

'It's time for me to get my contacts working,' said Brenner. 'I'm going to phone Griff and ask him to find the dog boys.'

Solomon looked at Brenner with an incredulous expression. Then he burst out laughing. 'Hold on,' he said. 'Let me get this straight, I have the might of the United States intelligence corps. The police, the CIA, black ops…but no, old Griff will find them. An ancient conspiracy nut with PTSD and clinical level of paranoia. Get real, Brenner.'

Brenner smiled. 'Yep,' insisted the big man. 'It's time to bring in the A-team.' He went to his pack, took out the satellite phone that linked him to his best friend and pushed the button to connect. He didn't care that it was five in the morning. Griff would be up by now at any rate.

The last time Brenner had seen Griff was when he had left to recuperate with an off-the-grid survivalist called Dave. As far as he knew, Griff was still there.

'It's five in the morning, you reprobate,' grunted the old man. 'Who phones anyone at five in the morning?'

'I do,' answered Brenner. 'And don't complain, I know you were awake, you been an early riser for as long as I've known you.'

'True,' admitted Griff. 'How's it hanging, big man, all things copasetic?'

So, Brenner told him. Everything. Starting with his sojourn in the mountain town of Backlash, the drug gangs, and finally, the *Hyaenidae Sapiens* and his new partnership with Solomon. The story took almost an hour.

At the end of the telling Griff asked if Solomon was in the room.

'Yep,' acknowledged Brenner.

'Put him on the phone,' demanded Griff.

The big man handed the phone over and Solomon held it to his ear.

'Hey, shit for brains, night crawling bastard,' said Griff. 'You bring any harm to my boy and I will find you and take you down. Trust me, I'm old and have nothing to lose, so heed my warning. Get it?'

'Got it,' replied Solomon and he handed the phone back.

'Give me twelve hours,' said Griff.

Brenner broke the connection and lit another cigarette.

'He cares for you,' said Solomon.

Brenner shrugged.

'Yeah, he does,' continued the man in black. 'He even threatened me,' he continued with a smile. 'Got balls, I'll give him that.'

Brenner grinned back. 'That he has, sir. That he has.'

CHAPTER 29

The colonel controlled his urge to stand up and smack doctor Mengele across his smug face. The Ex-Nazi took great pleasure in presenting his work to the colonel, or any colleague for that matter, in such a complicated fashion it ensured the recipient had no chance of following the methodology. This would force them to ask questions the doctor would answer with a sigh and an eye roll, as if he were a teacher addressing a special needs class.

It was a crude power play and, after almost fifty years of it, the colonel was beyond irritable.

But the doctor was essential to the Bloodborn Project, and the Americans had gone to great lengths in both rescuing the doctor from post war Germany and faking his subsequent death for the public. Because, truth be told, the man was a genius. And he had shown the project that it was amazing how you could get results if you literally didn't give a flying fuck about the wellbeing of your test subjects.

Results became the be all and end all, and morality took a place so far back in the line, it was no longer even an issue.

'Simplify, doctor,' commanded the colonel. 'And keep it brief. What exactly are you saying.'

'I am saying, my colonel, we have had a breakthrough. Using the strands of DNA from the *Hyaenidae Sapiens*, and combining them with *canis lupus familiaris,* specifically the Beagle, we have created a more subservient strain, while still retaining the utility and combat effectiveness of the *Hyaenidae*.'

'So, you crossed the hyena men with a dog?'

Mengele frowned. 'Well, yes, I suppose so. But it is far more complex than you make it sound. It's not baking, you know, it is the most advanced genetic manipulation ever practiced by man. It is genius.'

'Yes,' agreed the colonel. 'What next?'

'I need more subjects.'

'I just brought you in a truckload,' said the colonel. 'Courtesy of the witnesses of the bank raids we covered up.'

Mengele nodded. 'Yes. I have already used those up. The rate of attrition remains extremely high. Can you get another couple of truck loads? Men, young, mid-twenties at most.'

'I'll see what I can do,' answered the colonel.

'I need them sooner, rather than later,' insisted Mengele. 'These things have a rhythm, you know. A pace we must keep up with.'

'I said I will see what I can do,' repeated the colonel. 'Dismissed, doctor.'

The German bowed and left the room.

***

'Talk to me,' said Brenner as he answered the satellite phone.

'Found your dog boys,' said Griff. 'Well, I think I have. Maybe.'

'You have, or you haven't?' asked Brenner.

'Good chance I have. I put the word out on the dark net as well as all the conspiracy sites, the movers, and shakers. Everyone. The dudes are lapping it up. It's exactly the sort of thing we've been trying to warn everyone about for years now. Black ops government agency conducts illegal experiments and tries to cover up the results. Fucking meat and potatoes, man. The guys are all over it like ugly on a moose.'

Brenner smiled. It had been a while since he had heard Griff so excited over something. The old man was enjoying himself. 'Point, Griff,' he urged. 'Times wasting, you know. Places to go and people to kill.'

'Sure,' said Griff. 'Sorry. There's been another two bank raids. Same MO. The one took place in Trenton, Nebraska. Afterwards they split and went dark. Rumored to be travelling in a white Ford transit passenger wagon. Now, here's the thing, one of the boys on the net has spotted them. Looks like they took a couple of hits during the raid and they've stopped outside a little rural nothing town called, Stopgap. It's around sixty miles west of Trenton. They are currently on a farm on the main road on the way out of the town. The farm is called O'Reilly Stud. Fancy name, but it's basically a dirt farm.

Used to run horses but it's faded away to a subsistence and odd job plot. An old couple live there. My source reckons the bad dudes have taken the place over. He's a youngster so doesn't want to get involved.'

'Fair enough,' answered Brenner. 'So, you think this info is good?'

'It's good,' acknowledged Griff. 'Not golden, but still solid. Worth a bet.'

'We're on our way,' said Brenner. 'Four hours, maybe less. Thanks, Griff.'

'I'll keep on it,' said the old man. 'Good hunting.'

Brenner rang off.

CHAPTER 30

They arrived an hour before sundown, pulling to the side of the road about half a mile from their final destination, the O'Reilly Stud farm.

'We go the rest of the way on foot,' said Brenner. Then he turned to Shadow. 'I want you to stay here. There's a world of hurt waiting for us at the farm.'

Shadow simply shook her head and pointed at Brenner.

'There's no way she's going to stay here,' said Solomon. 'She'll be right on your six all the time. That's why she's called Shadow. Live with it.'

The big man sighed in acceptance. 'Fine. As soon as the sun goes down we move. Fast and silent. Do a recce of the perimeter, see if the dog boys are still there, and check for weak points in their defense.'

An hour later the four of them were crouched in a copse of trees overlooking the farmhouse. The area had once been fully fenced but the perimeter had long since broken down into a few desultory poles with rusted fingers of wire attached.

Brenner, Solomon, and Shadow were unarmed but Howard carried an ACR Bushmaster rifle with a Viper night scope.

The farmhouse itself was painted a faded red, as were the barns. All the structures were dilapidated and dirty. The yard around the house was overgrown, and two old Ford Fairmont's, circa 1970 stood on bricks in front of the door.

Brenner could smell livestock. Cows. But no dogs. Although the rank stench of the *Hyaenidae* cut through the air like dog crap in a church.

There were four guards posted around the house. One at each corner, patrolling back and forth over a small designated area. They each carried an M16A4 assault rifle and appeared to be alert. None were smoking, they walked their beat methodically and kept a constant check on the perimeter.

Brenner pointed at them. 'We take them down first,' he whispered. 'Solomon, you go right, I'll go left. Howard, overwatch.

Any surprise participants, take them out. After that, check out the windows. See if the civilians are still alive and kicking. Check the layout, positions of the rest of the gang, pay special attention to the dog boys. Then we either come back here to plan, or attack straight away. Let's see what presents itself.'

'Typical Brenner strategy,' said Solomon. 'See people, kill people, scratch ass, go home.'

'Got any better suggestions?' asked the big man.

Solomon shook his head.

'Well then can it,' snapped Brenner. 'Let's go.'

Both Howard and the man in black nodded.

Brenner didn't bother to give Shadow any instructions. He knew she would be right behind him.

Howard took up his position while Brenner and Solomon split up and approached the guards.

Shadow ghosted along behind Brenner but, just like the two supernatural warriors, she was one with the darkness. Silent and ethereal.

The guards died in silence. Brenner breaking necks and Solomon severing jugulars with swift, razor-sharp claws.

But as Brenner put down the second guard, a fifth one rose unseen from a hide behind one of the cars, raising his rifle as he did so. The big man turned hard and fast but, before he could move, there was a flicker of movement and a soft gurgle of sound as Shadow ghosted past him and struck, slamming her extended fingers into the man's throat. He sank to the floor, holding his smashed esophagus as he drowned in his own blood.

She smiled at Brenner's incredulous look then pointed at one of the windows. The big man shook off his shock and moved on, continuing with his recce.

The farmhouse was large and sprawling. None of the windows had drapes but, due to the dust and dirt, they were not easy to see through.

Brenner moved quickly but quietly, peering in at each window. Most of the rooms were empty. The third window answered the question regarding the whereabouts and condition of the original occupants. The room inside was a charnel house. Blood covered the walls and even the ceiling. Various dismembered body parts lay carelessly scattered about. A foot, a head. Ropes of intestines and random wet chunks of flesh. It was impossible to make a guess at how many had died as most of the bodies had been consumed, the teeth marks obvious. Torn and shredded flesh, splintered bones, and half-masticated bits.

Shadow growled softly, and Brenner felt his ire rise. Inside him, the wolf threw itself against the bars of its new prison and howled for release.

'Kill. Kill them all,' it screamed. *'Kill the dogs. Kill the troopers. Kill Howard.'*

But Brenner forced its thoughts down, shuddering as he imposed his humanity over the beast inside.

Shadow stroked his back and looked at him with an expression of concern, raising an eyebrow in question.

The big man shook his head. 'No worries,' he whispered. 'Let's keep looking.'

There were two more windows on his side of the house and they were both in the same room. A large living area. The rest of the stormtroopers and the two dog boys were in the room. Brenner picked out the permanent with ease. Even though his hood covered his face, he was easy to spot. Massively hunched back, legs that bent the wrong way, and a high odor that was identifiable even from outside the window.

The second *Hyaenidae* wasn't as obvious, but he also had the hunched back muscle and his eyes were deep yellow and bloodshot. His scent also pervaded the atmosphere. Rotting meat and wet dog fur.

Brenner ducked down and slid away from the building, turning to Shadow as he did. 'Back to the rendezvous point,' he whispered. 'Let's make a plan on how to take this bunch out.'

But as he spoke, one of the windows shattered outwards as the permanent *Hyaenidae* sprung through it. Brenner's surveillance obviously hadn't been as undetectable as he had thought, and he turned to face the enemy with a curse.

Brenner was fast. Faster than almost any other living thing on the planet. But the permanent hit him before he had time to set himself. And it was like being run over by a Mack truck. He felt his ribs crack and break and his intercostal muscles tear as he was shunted backwards.

Shadow yowled and jumped on the dog boy's back, clawing at his eyes, and kicking his torso. But he simply reached over his shoulder, grabbed her, and threw her at least thirty feet away. She twisted in the air as she flew, landing on her feet and sprinting straight back at the animal person.

At the same time, the front door burst open and the stormtroopers ran out. But Howard had them covered, and the vicious crack of his rifle announced his presence. The troopers hit the ground, seeking cover, scuttling away from the accurate fire. By the time they had lost themselves in the night, Howard had dispatched three of them.

The permanent picked Brenner up and smashed a fist into his face, breaking his nose with an audible crunch. The big man twisted out of the *Hyaenidae's* grip and returned the punch, hitting hard and fast with both hands. It felt like he was hitting a concrete wall, but the blows did have some effect, driving the dog boy back and causing him to flinch slightly.

Then, Shadow was on its back again, clawing and biting and screaming in anger. At the same time, Solomon appeared like a magic trick. One moment he wasn't there, the next he was standing next to the *Hyaenidae* unleashing a barrage of strikes to coincide with Brenner's attack.

The permanent backhanded the man in black. The blow lifted Solomon off his feet and smashed him into a nearby tree with bone-breaking force. The tree shuddered, and the sound of his back breaking competed with his scream of pain. But even as he slid to the ground, the formula that raged through his body was repairing the damage, knitting back the shattered bones and severed nerve endings.

Brenner wasn't doing as well. Although his body regenerated many times quicker than a normal human's, it was only in Wolfman mode that he became close to immortal, repairing horrific injuries in seconds. But his strength and speed, although off the charts, were not even close to the abilities he boasted when in wolf mode.

And he was paying the price for refusing to change.

His left arm dangled by his side, broken in at least six places. His jaw was unhinged, shattered by the *Hyaenidae's* jackhammer blows, and he was bleeding profusely from a deep bite on his left shoulder.

'Change,' yelled Solomon. 'Change or we all die.'

But Brenner shook his head. He knew if he changed now he wouldn't have the strength of character to change back. The formula that Solomon had injected him with had robbed him of his humanity, and once the wolf was free it would never come home to civilization again. It would kill and kill and kill. Worse than the *Hyaenidae*. Worse than the worst nightmares.

So, he took a deep breath and attacked the permanent again, redoubling his efforts, as did both Shadow and Solomon. Cuts were opening up in the dog boys flesh as the repeated blows from both Brenner and Solomon made their way through its defense. And Shadow's nonstop attacks on the things eyes started to pay off, as its one eye swelled shut.

Finally, under the combined savagery

being dealt to it, the *Hyaenidae* broke and ran, it's inherent cowardice winning out over its physical strength and ability.

But before it bolted, it dealt out one last flurry of kicks and bites and punches, scattering its three assailants, breaking Brenner's right leg, tossing Solomon into a tree again and dislodging Shadow from his back.

Then he was gone.

Howard appeared out of the darkness, his Bushmaster rifle at the ready. 'They've gone,' he said. 'Two of them took off in a Ford, tried to stop them but the angle wasn't good, put a few holes in the bodywork but that's all. I killed all the troopers. Also managed to get in a couple of shots on the guy you were fighting, but no effect. He just shrugged them off.'

'Yeah,' grunted Brenner. 'Those dog boys are bulletproof mother fuckers. Ain't never seen the like.'

Shadow knelt next to the big man and stroked his head, peering at his wounds with concern.

Brenner gave her a tight grin. 'Don't fuss,' he said. 'I'll heal up soon. Just let me sit here for a couple more minutes.' He turned to Solomon. 'You OK?'

'It was a humbling experience,' answered the man in black. 'Can't say I enjoyed it in any way or form. I knew they were tough, but that was off the scale.' He looked at Shadow. 'And there's more to you than meets the eye, missy.'

'I reckon we go find a hotel,' said Brenner. 'Catch some serious R&R and formulate a plan. Maybe something a little more sophisticated than my usual, see them and knock them down MO.'

'You think?' asked Solomon with a grin.

'Yeah,' admitted Brenner ruefully. 'I think.'

CHAPTER 31

They booked into the Montrose Hotel in Trenton at four-thirty that morning. More upmarket than Brenner would have gone for, but not fancy enough to stop Solomon turning his nose up and shaking his head.

'Needs must,' he muttered as he paid for the rooms, once again putting Brenner and Shadow together.

Shadow showered first, then Brenner. By the time the big man had finished, the girl was already asleep, head buried beneath her blanket as usual.

Solomon knocked at one o'clock that afternoon and Brenner let him in. The man in black sat at the small table, pulling up one of the three chairs. Shadow was already seated and was polishing off what looked like the remains of a breakfast for six, the empty plates and glasses stacked together like the detritus from a military mess hall.

'Do you think your old man can find

them again?' he asked Brenner without any preamble.

'His name is Griff,' noted Brenner. 'And, yes. If they're moving, he can find them.'

'Good. I've made a few calls, organized us upgraded ordnance. Some super serious firepower, heavy enough to take down a tank. So next time we go up against these hyena boys we can sort them out. We need to get to Kansas City. It's a couple of hundred clicks from here. Shouldn't take us long. Got a meet at The Knucklehead Bar & Grill on the outskirts. You should like the place, it's a real shit hole.'

Brenner sighed. 'If it's all the same to you,' he said. 'I won't be coming.'

'Why?' asked Solomon. 'You sick?'

'No. It's just, whenever I'm in this situation, things go to shit. We'll pitch up at the bar, for no reason at all, someone will come over and offer to kick my ass. I'll respond, and that's the end of a civilized evening. Griff says it's because I'm some sort of dickhead magnet. I attract assholes like dog crap attracts flies.'

'Wow,' exclaimed Solomon. 'I find that hard to believe, what with your winning personality and gentle nature. Tell you what, I need backup, so you need to come, but, and here's the thing, sit quietly, don't eyeball anyone, and don't act like a condescending shit. That should sort out the whole asshole magnet ability.'

The big man shrugged. 'Fine. Don't say I didn't warn you.'

'Whatever,' responded Solomon. 'It's a six-hour drive, let's move.'

Howard drove Solomon in the BMW and Brenner and Shadow followed on the Harley rat bike. They drove fast, well over the limit, relying on both Brenner's and Solomon's unique senses to spot traps and police in time to slow down to legal speeds.

After a single stop for food, they made the trip in just under five hours, hitting the bar an hour after sundown.

As was the usual method, Howard stayed outside as overwatch and the rest wandered into the bar.

Brenner felt right at home. Neon beer ads buzzed on the walls, two pool tables dominated the room, both with cigarette burns on the baize. Men with beards, girls with tight jeans and tighter crop tops.

Cigarette smoke, spilled beer, and chili.

Shadow scoped the place with a scowl, while Solomon shook his head in amusement as he walked over to the bar. 'I'll get some Scotch,' he said.

'You wish,' countered Brenner.

'True,' admitted the man in black. 'Some Jack then.'

Shadow pointed at the door to the restroom and left.

Brenner stood for a while and simply took in the atmosphere. Then he saw them, and it felt like someone had thrown a bucket of cold water over him.

'You gotta be shitting me,' he said to himself as he walked over to the table in the corner.

Both were dark-skinned with long gray hair and blue eyes. Bushy gray beards, semiformal clothing. Open necked white shirts, dark suits, and patent leather shoes. Their clothes were neat and clean, but so threadbare you could almost pick out the individual strands of the weave.

As Brenner approached, they raised their shot glasses in greeting and poured one for him.

'Mister Reeve. Mister Bolin.'

'Wolfman.'

'To what do I owe the dubious pleasure?' asked Brenner.

'We need to talk,' said Mister Reeve.

'I thought you didn't do talk,' said Brenner. 'I thought it was all watching and no interaction.'

'Mister Bolin rocked his hand back and forth. '*Comme ci, comme ca*,' he said. 'There are no hard and fast rules.'

'Speak then,' said Brenner.

'You need to change,' said Mister Bolin. 'Unless you do, all is lost. You are the only one who can go up against these hyena abominations and win. But only if you change. Only if you assume your true form.'

Brenner sneered at the two old men. 'Really? You think? You know what the problem is with you two? You watch, but you don't see. You witness but you don't perceive. You mistake observation with insight. I cannot change. Not anymore. If I change, I will lose control. And if I lose control I will make those hyena things look like a puppy fest. They at least have some sort of a plan, no matter that it is warped and twisted. If I change, the Wolfman will have no plan, no long-term strategy. He will have only one goal. Kill.

'Kill everyone. Kill everything. I know. I have felt it and it is terrifying. So, don't come to me with, "you must change". Anyway, Solomon has organized us some heavy hardware. Next time we meet with these animals, we take them out. End of story.'

Both of the old men shook their heads.

'If you do not change, then all is lost,' said Mister Bolin. And, for the first time, Brenner saw a look of despair on the ancient's face. A look of loss. Defeat, even. 'Lost,' he repeated.

Brenner felt a tug on his shirt and turned to see Shadow had joined him. 'Hi,' he said. 'Just chatting to these old dudes here,' he told her as he pointed at an empty table.

Shadow looked puzzled, then she simply shrugged and pulled at Brenner's shirt again, tugging him with her as she walked away, heading for a doorway next to the restrooms. Brenner didn't bother asking where they were going as he knew she wouldn't answer. Best simply follow and it would all become self-explanatory.

She opened the door and walked in, still pulling Brenner with her.

A smaller room. In the middle, a card table. Four men sat around it. Poker. Five card draw. Another twelve men sat at a small bar at the far end of the room and a bevy of females in the obligatory tight jeans and tops were scattered about the room like jewels in dirt.

One of the men at the table looked up. 'Private room,' he said, and went back to looking at his cards.

Brenner looked at Shadow, trying to get a feed from her as to what she had dragged him in for.

One of the other men detached himself from the bar and lumbered over. He was obvious muscle. As tall as Brenner, wider, muscle covered by a layer of fat. Beard to his chest, A tattoo of a bat wrapped around his neck, its fangs buried in his jugular, bright red blood, and white teeth. A real work of art.

'Private,' he repeated. 'That means, you get the fuck out.'

He made as if to push Brenner in the chest, but Shadow slapped his hand away and pushed him instead. He staggered backwards with a look of utter incredulity on his face as the tiny woman's incongruous strength registered. It was like a pixie pushing a troll.

Shadow plucked at Brenner's shirt again and pointed to the corner.

The big man looked hard. There was a group of three women sitting together. But their features were difficult to make out as the lighting was low, and that particular corner was even duller than the rest of the room.

But as he concentrated he could see the one woman had a large bruise stamped across her face. Also, a swollen eye and a split lip. Someone had gone to town on her, to the point that there was most likely further unseen damage. Perhaps a broken nose, loose teeth. Maybe even a cracked jaw.

Then Shadow pointed at the man at the card table who had first addressed Brenner. After that, she folded her arms and raised a quizzical eyebrow. Her message was obvious.

Brenner sighed. 'Fucking asshole magnet,' he said under his breath as he approached the table. 'Hey, you.' He poked the man in the back of his head with his forefinger. 'Wanna explain why the lady in the corner looks like she's just gone ten rounds with Tyson Fury?'

The man stood and spun around. 'What the fuck? You looking to commit suicide, boy?' he shouted. 'Because you going about it the right way.'

Brenner decided that whatever happened next, the end game would be the same. The asshat who had punched the girl would tell Brenner to fuck off. The rest of the gang would surround him and, they would all strive to kick the living crap out of him.

So, he cut to the chase. Leaning forward, he grabbed the dude by his crotch and his neck, lifted him above his head and threw him down on the card table, reducing it to kindling. Then he proceeded to pick the man up again, this time by his shirt front, and slap him. Forehand, backhand, forehand. 'With each blow he imparted some sage advice.

'Don't,' slap. 'Hit,' slap. 'Girls,' slap. 'You,' slap. 'Bully,' slap.

The man's friends all piled in like extras in a low budget Western movie; all fists and feet.

Shadow ran over to the girl in the corner and stood over her, protecting her from any collateral damage.

And Brenner, née Wolfman, set about doing what he was best at. He dropped the unconscious first offender and turned his attention to the rest of the gang. Furniture flew, and glasses were smashed as the big man waded through the opposition, swinging his fists like twin wrecking balls.

Halfway through the fight, Solomon entered the room, carrying three glasses of Jack. He walked over to the bar, sat, and watched, the ghost of a smile on his face.

And Brenner suddenly realized he was actually enjoying himself. He was dealing out justice to a gang of bullies. But they were humans. Complete with all their weaknesses and foibles. It wasn't a life-threatening, world-ending situation, involving hybrid supernaturals and black ops and underground government conspiracies.

It was merely a bit of physical explanation. A good old-fashioned bar brawl.

He looked over at Shadow and grinned.

She gave him a thumbs up, instinctively understanding that he wasn't reveling in the violence. Instead he was rejoicing in the absolute normality of the situation.

Two men and a girl walk into a bar ... and none of them are werewolves.

Brenner finally cuffed the last man to the floor and sauntered over to Solomon who handed him a drink.

'I see you've got your asshole magnet turned up to maximum,' noted the man in black.

Brenner laughed. 'And then some.'

Shadow walked over with the injured girl in tow.

The girl nodded at Brenner. 'Thanks,' she said. 'I suppose. Not sure what I'm going to do when he wakes up, though. He's gonna be real pissed at me. Probably beat me up some more.'

Solomon went over to the vanquished boyfriend and quickly frisked him, coming away with a thick wad of cash and a set of keys. He handed them to the girl.

'Looks like a couple of grand there,' he said. 'Plus, some car keys. If I were you I would leave that asshole, go find a new life. Who needs this?' he gestured around him, 'Or, if you want, I could just kill him and then you'd have no problem.'

The girl laughed, then stopped when she realized Solomon wasn't joking. 'No,' she said. 'No killing. I mean, he's a real SOB, but death is pretty harsh. I think I'll just take his stash and his Mustang and leave.'

She nodded her farewell and left, pausing only to deliver a number of full-blooded kicks to the fallen man's head, opening up a few more cuts to add to the myriad he already had.

'Come on,' said Solomon. 'Drink up. My contact is waiting for us in the carpark. And I think that we should conclude our business ASAP, then clear out before this lot wake up and we are forced to make a more permanent example of them.'

The three trooped out of the bar. The rest of the patrons noted them leave but took care not to stare or comment, lest they feel the wrath of the big man who grinned while he fought.

Outside, parked next to the BMW, was a 1961 Park Avenue Cadillac in pristine condition. A man lounged against the passenger door. Short, wide, swarthy. Goatee, gold teeth, and a too small fedora on his bald head.

'Paco,' greeted Solomon. 'I see you still driving that ancient piece of shit.'

'Hey, fuck you, man,' responded the fedora wearer. 'It's a classic. And at least I buy American.'

'Sure,' said the man in black. 'You got my goods?'

The short man walked around to the trunk and popped it to reveal two long black boxes and a few smaller cardboard ones. 'Take a look.'

Solomon nodded his head at Howard, and the driver stepped forward, opened one of the long boxes and took out the contents.

It was a Boys anti-tank rifle, capable of firing a .55 round through an inch of steel plate.

Paco grabbed one of the small boxes and opened it up. He extracted a single round. It was massive. Longer than his hand and almost half as thick as his wrist. 'Had these specially made up for you,' he said to Solomon. 'Titanium tipped. This thing will go straight through an entire engine block and still have enough residual energy to kill anyone on the other side.'

Solomon smiled. 'Nice. Now let's see what happens when the dog boys try to stand up against this.'

'You want both rifles and all of the ammo?' asked Paco.

'Sure,' said Solomon. 'Put them in the BMW, I'll have the money transferred into the usual account.'

The two of them shook hands. Paco climbed into his Cadillac and left without a backward glance.

'Hey, Brenner,' said Solomon, just before he got into the BMW. 'I was thinking. Has it ever occurred to you, maybe, just maybe, you're not an asshole magnet? Maybe you're the actual asshole in all those situations you find yourself in?'

Shadow growled at the man in black, but Brenner simply smiled.

'You know what,' he said. 'I reckon you might be right.'

CHAPTER 32

The next three days were spent waiting.

Usually, Brenner would be going out of his mind from boredom but, for some reason, he was fine, simply sitting in the hotel room, watching endless reruns of eighties television, and eating industrial quantities of food.

Perhaps it was Shadow's presence. Her calm demeanor, her comfortable silence, and obvious devotion to him, provided a much-needed salve for his soul.

On the third day, Griff phoned. It was late evening.

'Got them,' he said by way of greeting. 'They did another bank yesterday. The town of Price, Utah. But one of my contacts has spotted them hiding out in the Uintah and Ouray Indian Reservation. I'm going to send you the map coordinates. There are tracks to the place, but it's not on any maps. Close to the Ashley National forest. You're looking at a ten-hour drive.

Maybe eight if you put the pedal to the metal.'

'Thanks, Griff.'

Twelve minutes later, they were on the road and heading west at top speed.

They arrived at their destination at sun up.

Solomon raised the heavily tinted partition between the driver and passenger compartment and sat in the back of the BMW, grumbling about UV rays and the dire consequences to exposure thereof. Howard stayed seated in the driver's seat, awaiting any orders or instructions.

Brenner and Shadow stood next to the Harley and drank in the view. The sun rose over distant mountains, a giant red orb that stained the sky with blood. Quaking Aspen trees carpeted the foreground and, sparkling in amongst the vegetation, a small river splashed and tumbled its way south.

Shadow grasped Brenner's hand and the two of them stood in silence for a minute, letting nature flow through them.

The big man opened his wolf-senses and let them roam, picking up elk, moose, coyotes and even bear. The wolf growled and howled internally. *Kill them*, it urged.

But the feeling of the tiny hand in his helped him force the thoughts of violence away, soothing them with the sweet balm that was Shadow.

Then Brenner was distracted by the sound of the BMW passenger window being wound down.

'You two going to gawk at mother nature all day, or are you going to do some killing?' asked Solomon.

Howard opened his door and got out of the limousine, going around the back and popping the trunk.

'I think we should go for a Brenner-style plan,' continued Solomon from the inside of the vehicle. 'Find the dog boys and their storm troopers, do a bit of a recce, shoot the hyenas, kill the rest, come back, we go home. Or at least decamp to another hotel and wait for the old man to update us. Obviously, I cannot help here due to my fragile constitution regarding daylight. Are we agreed?'

'I'm not going to tell you again,' said Brenner. 'His name is, Griff. He doesn't like being called, old. And that was your last warning.'

'Lighten up, big man,' said Solomon. 'He can't hear us.'

'It's the principle,' insisted Brenner. 'Griff, or Mister Griffin, or Reece. Not old man, old dude, or old timer.'

Solomon was about to voice some sort of come back, when he saw Brenner's expression and noted the big man was deadly serious. 'Fine,' he said, biting his tongue. 'Mister Griffin it is then.'

Brenner nodded. 'Thank you.'

Howard took the two Boys rifles out of the trunk, removing them from their boxes first. He handed one to Brenner then both of them proceeded to strip them down, checking each component as they did so. A few minutes later they were ready to rock and roll.

Brenner took a last quick look at the satnav, got his bearings, and took point, loping towards their destination with long strides. Howard kept up, running hard. But Shadow, even though she was so small, ran next to him with ease, as quiet and insubstantial as her *nom de guerre* implied.

As it turned out, the dog boys were not difficult to find. Their scent lay heavy over the area like a miasma and Brenner homed in on them with relative ease, even though they had covered the Ford with camo netting and their tents were small and green, blending in with the surrounding forest.

They had pitched camp in a small hollow, next to a stream and in amongst a thick copse of Aspen trees. Brenner had led them to a hill overlooking the camp, some two hundred yards away. He had also ensured he was downwind, assuming the *Hyaenidae* had a sense of smell comparable to his.

The three of them lay flat and observed the camp for half an hour before Brenner whispered to Howard.

'What do you think?'

'Amateur hour,' replied the driver. 'Three guards, not even scanning their surrounds. Everyone else acting like it's a boy scout jamboree. I can't see the head *Hyaenidae Sapiens*. He must be in one of the tents, but the permanent is over there by the stream.'

'Yep, I concur,' said Brenner. 'I think we take out the dog boy by the river first, then hope that flushes out the chief hyena. Take him out as soon as we see him. After that, I get up close and personal with the rest. Keep one alive to get some info regarding their HQ.'

Howard nodded. 'Simple. Doable. Let's go for it.'

'No time like the present,' agreed Brenner.

The two men adjusted their positions slightly and lined up the huge rifles on their target.

'You take the first shot,' said Brenner. 'Then I'll take a backup one if needed.'

Howard, peered through his scope, let out his breath and stroked the trigger.

The sound of the massive round discharging was obscenely loud as it shattered the quiet peace of the forest.

Flocks of birds exploded from the treetops, small game broke and ran through the underbrush and every head swiveled around, looking for the source.

But most importantly, the permanent *Hyaenidae* lifted off his feet and thumped into a nearby tree, as the .55-inch armor piercing round struck it in the chest at a speed of over three thousand feet per second, imparting almost fifteen thousand-foot pounds of pressure. Enough kinetic energy to literally stop a WW2 main battle tank in its tracks.

Brenner couldn't stop a huge grin suffusing his face and he pat Howard on the shoulder. 'Good shot,' he said.

Howard nodded back at him.

Shadow interrupted the two of them by punching Brenner in the shoulder and pointing.

The permanent was standing up and shaking its head. A trickle of blood ran down its chest but, apart from that, it seemed unaffected.

Without a pause, Brenner sighted up and squeezed off a round. The projectile struck the monster center mass, right next to the previous shot. Again, the thing was thrown backwards by the massive amount of power that had been imparted to it.

Once again, it stood, slightly disoriented, but otherwise unaffected.

Howard fired again. Head shot. The permanent flicked backwards and he did a full somersault before hitting the ground. This time, he lay still for almost three seconds before staggering to his feet.

By now the storm troopers had gotten an idea where the shots were coming from and they were laying down withering sheets of fire in return.

And while the Boys antitank rifle has awesome stopping power, it was slow and cumbersome to aim and reload. In fact, it was exactly the wrong weapon for taking on multiple targets at relatively close range.

'Sir,' said Howard, his normally calm voice betraying a touch of stress. 'I recommend we make a strategic withdrawal.'

'If by that you mean we cut and run,' answered Brenner. 'Then I fully agree. Let's get the fuck out of here.'

The trio sprinted back to the vehicles, throwing the rifles into the BMW trunk as soon as they arrived.

'Hey, what gives? asked Solomon.

'It's a wash,' answered Brenner. 'All these rifles do is piss them off. And now they're coming for us. Hard and fast. It's time to get the hell of Dodge while the getting's still good.'

The BMW pulled off with the Harley right behind it.

And the two vehicles kept up a top speed until they were well clear of the forest and surrounds.

***

Howard booked them into the Hilton in the town of St. George, Utah. Three rooms.

After unpacking, they all gathered in Solomon's room and ordered room service. No one had spoken on the drive from the reservation, and Howard had simply driven until nightfall then pulled in to the first decent hotel they had come across.

The food arrived, and they started eating.

'Well that was unexpected,' said Brenner, the first to broach the subject. 'Who would have thought those dogs were totally bulletproof?'

No one responded.

Eventually Solomon spoke, leaning back in his chair first and blowing out an exaggerated sigh. 'You know, Brenner,' he said. 'When I contacted you because I needed your help to put this threat down, I thought I was contacting the Wolfman. I thought I was teaming up with a weapon of mass destruction. Not some washed out old

Vietnam, vet with PTSD, and a new-found respect for human life, tree hugging and safe fucking spaces for everyone.'

'What are you saying?' asked Brenner.

'What? I'm not being clear enough for you? Unless you change, big man, then you're nothing but dead weight. I hired a gunslinger and I got the town hippie instead. To take those dog boys out, you have to go wolf. And fuck the collateral damage. Needs must, Brenner.'

Shadow stood and growled at Solomon, but the man in black simply grinned back at her. 'Watch that attitude, girl,' he said. 'Uncle Solomon has had about enough of your shit for now. Want to go for me? Try. Or shut the fuck up.'

Shadow glanced at Brenner, but the big man shook his head and she sat.

'You want the truth?' he asked Solomon.

Solomon nodded. 'That would be nice.'

'The truth is,' continued Brenner. 'After what I've seen, I'm not sure the Wolfman could take those *Hyaenidae*.'

'The colonel reckons you could,' countered Solomon.

'What the hell does the colonel know?

Nothing,' snapped Brenner.

'Bullshit,' said Solomon. 'The colonel knows everything. Shit, man. They've been studying the info they have on you for over fifty years now. They know things about you you don't know. And if the colonel says the Wolfman can take the dogs, then he's most likely correct. Asshole that he is.'

Brenner shrugged. 'Not sure about that.'

'Hey, don't go soft on me now, big man,' urged Solomon. 'We need you at top form if we're going to stop these abominations killing more people.'

'From where I sit, they aren't our biggest problem,' said Brenner. 'From what I can see, they've killed a few people, but the colonel has killed hundreds more covering his own ass. So, who's the evil one in the scenario? The *Hyaenidae,* who are pretty much doing what they have been programmed to do. Programmed by the Project.

'Or the colonel, who is killing hundreds, if not thousands of innocent Americans to stop the world finding out about his fuck up?'

'One battle at a time,' said Solomon.

'Basic military strategy. We take care of the dog boys, then we take care of the colonel.'

'What do you mean, take care of the colonel?' asked Brenner. 'He's your boss. Your hero.'

The man in black shook his head, his eyes showing his distress. 'Not any more,' he said, his voice barely above a whisper. 'He's gone too far this time. Women, children. Entire families. He's lost the plot and we're the only ones who can stop him. But first, the dog boys. Then their master.'

Brenner nodded. 'OK. Let me think this through. I'll tell Griff to keep looking. If the wolf is the only way to go, then so be it. But I want Howard and a Boys rifle keeping overwatch at all time. And if I wig out, he shoots me in the head. Deal?'

Solomon frowned.

'Deal? Asked Brenner again as he held his hand out.

Solomon sighed and took the big man's hand. 'Deal.'

CHAPTER 33

'The time draws close,' said Anubis as he stood proud in front of his people. 'We have the weapons and we have the funds. Now the Sons will strike and strike hard. In one day we will make a difference to the entire world. Everyone shall know that the Sons of One Eight are a force to be respected. A force of change in the world.'

'Death to the Muslims,' shouted the Sons. 'Burn the mosques. Kill the imams.'

Anubis held up his hands for silence. 'Yes,' he agreed to the fervent shouts. 'The Muslims must suffer. And the Jews. But we are not here to strike petty blows against single buildings and individual people. We are here to change the world.'

The Sons cheered and the *Hyaenidae* howled their pleasure and excitement.

'This weekend there is an international trade summit being held in Los Angeles. Companies from the United Kingdom, Russia and Germany will be attending the trade show at the L.A. Conference Center. Billeted nearby, in three separate hotels, will be the UK prime minister, the German chancellor and the president of the Russian Federation.'

Anubis paused for more cheering, and some came, although it was muted. He knew it would be so, as he knew his troopers were wondering what the three leaders he had just mentioned had to do with exterminating the Muslim threat.

'What do they have to do with the Muslims?' continued the head *Hyaenidae*. 'Why attack them? Let me tell you.'

The thing that the Bloodborn Project had created strode across the stage, it's movements fluid as silk, awash with power. Yellow eyes glimmering with barely leashed insanity, the hunched muscles on its back writhing like a sack of pythons as it moved.

'Intelligence officers in the United Kingdom have identified twenty-three thousand jihadist extremists living in the country. But they do nothing about it. Nothing. They don't even bother to watch them. Thousands of these jihadis have left the United Kingdom to join ISIS, and when they come home, they're still not imprisoned.

'The mayor of their largest city, London, has written a book entitled "Actions Against the Police," in which he details how to sue the police for "racism". The same mayor has openly defended the 9/11 terrorists. Openly and without reprimand or shame.

'British born jihadis have been responsible for more deaths and terrorist acts in America than either Yemen, Syria, Somalia, Libya, Iraq, Kuwait and the UAE. And the people of England and her prime minister do nothing. For this, they must be punished.

'Germany have opened their borders to Muslims, welcoming them without any form of security check whatsoever, and now over a million live in the fatherland, raping and stealing from good Aryan people. The government spend half of NATO's recommended amount on their military, allowing the might of the Bundeswehr to dwindle until it is no longer even a viable army. For this they must be punished.

'Russia is dispatching weapons to the

Taliban. In Syria, Moscow's military campaign is not directed against Islamic State but is intended to annihilate the moderate opposition forces supported by the West. Moscow does not even view the Lebanese Shiite group, Hezbollah, as a terrorist organization. For this they must be punished.'

The cheering and howling had reached a climactic level as Anubis ranted, his lips flecked with foam, his arms held wide, muscles jumping and quivering in excess.

'And we are the ones to deliver the punishment,' finished the hyena man as he threw his head back and barked frantically.

CHAPTER 34

The British contingent arrived early morning and because the visit was billed as a three-day working visit, the only official appointment would be the flight line ceremony at the airport. The same rules would apply to both the Russian and the German parties.

On arrival at the airport, the prime minister, president, or chancellor would walk down the air stairs as the U.S. Air Force Band performed "Arrival Fanfare Number One". At the bottom of the stairs, he or she would then be greeted by an American schoolchild with a bouquet of flowers before being introduced to the welcoming committee by the chief of protocol. The national anthems of the visiting state and the United States would then be performed prior to the visitor's departure to their accommodations. During this time, they would all be accompanied by their entourage and security detail.

In the case of the United Kingdom, the entourage and security detail consisted of sixteen bodyguards, six politicians, the prime minister, and her two personal assistants.

The German chancellor arrived with a slightly smaller entourage including twelve bodyguards, six politicians and one assistant.

The Russian president arrived with one hundred and sixty-three people. No one seemed to be sure how many of those were bodyguards, politicians, assistants, or family.

Their arrivals were staggered throughout the morning and, by mid-day, all three parties had been ensconced in their respective accommodations.

The Brits at a luxury apartment block overlooking the center.

The Germans in a similar, but slightly more utilitarian block.

And the Russians, who had rented the top six floors of the five-star Ritz hotel.

***

The British prime minister gazed out of

the window at the skyline and tried to ignore the arguing of her advisors, assistants, and colleagues.

When she had first maneuvered herself into the job of leading her country she had been ecstatic. Years of backstabbing, lying, and conniving finally paying off.

Now, six months in, she was exhausted beyond belief. And she had come to realize that when you become top dog your entire existence became about keeping yourself at the top of the pile. The microscopic amount of time and energy available to actually do any good for the country was so negligible, that if anything did ever get done it was by coincidence rather than by plan.

In fact, it seemed as though her job, and indeed the jobs of everyone around her, was to simply condemn any competition in both her own party and the opposition party.

And everybody else's *raison d'être* was to simply oppose her. No one cared about the good of the country or its people. This was politics at its highest level, and the will of the people could go and fuck itself.

Still, one mustn't grumble, she thought

to herself as she took a deep breath and readied herself to call the room to order. But, before she could do so, one of her security detail barged in, a solemn look on his face.

'Ma'am,' he called out. 'There has been a serious breach of the perimeter. Two of the men are already down. We need to institute Protocol Churchill immediately.'

The prime minister blanched as the blood rushed from her face. Protocol Churchill was the highest level of alert for any attack. Basically, it meant, bend down, and kiss your own ass goodbye, because it's only a matter of time.

Suddenly the room was awash with running, shouting people. A security guard helped her into a full armoured outfit, complete with ceramic plates and Kevlar leggings. Assistants and advisors were ushered out of the room, some with physical force as they attempted to disagree and stay with her. Then another five security men ran in. First, they placed steel props against the door, then they picked up the beds and piled them against the entrance as well.

The prime minister's brain quickly did

the math. If two of her men were already down and six were in the room with her, that left another eight outside. Plus, the Los Angeles police and the usual contingent of SWAT, special forces and secret service agents that were assigned to any visiting dignitary.

Literally hundreds of heavily armed men with only one focus – protect the British prime minister.

With a sigh, she calmed her racing heart. Nothing short of a full military strike would get through that wall of steel.

She would be safe.

Guaranteed.

CHAPTER 35

'They're going to hit the trade fair,' said Griff as soon as Brenner answered the satellite phone. 'The one in Los Angeles.'

'Woah, slow down,' answered Brenner. 'What trade show? How? Why?'

'There's a trade show opening in the Los Angeles trade center this Friday,' explained Griff. 'It's one of those, "Hands across the ocean" crap. You know, we're all good friends in this global economy, I buy your crap and you buy mine.

'It features Russia, United Kingdom, and Germany. It's a big thing, our esteemed leader showing that the whole world loves him. The leaders of all the respective countries are going to give speeches there, meeting and greeting. Your basic political ass kissing meets corporate schmoozing. But as far as I can tell, they aren't going to be in the same room at any one time. It's not a summit, it's just a trade thing. So, if the dog boys wanna hit the leaders, it'll have to be done piecemeal or they'll need to split their teams up.'

'What are you basing this info on?' asked Brenner.

'Tons of stuff,' answered the old man. 'I have literally got thousands of hackers, conspiracy theorists, weekend reporters and concerned citizens working on this. They send me over a thousand messages a day, alleged sightings, theories, photos. Then I run the whole lot through a program I wrote called "Big Sister". She narrows the whole mess down using keyword analysis, preset algorithms, and inbuilt parameters. After that, I manually check the results.

'Didn't take long to figure the Sons of One Eight are using two or three white Ford transit passenger wagons to ferry themselves to and from the bank robberies. I even got partial number plates. Then all I did was inform everyone about that fact, add in their suspected numbers, last known locations, possible routes to and from … wasn't actually that difficult.'

'How come Homeland Security and the FBI couldn't do it then?' asked Brenner.

'Because they don't have Reece Griffin

working for them,' laughed the old man. 'Oh, and also because they're a bunch of procedure bound idiots who are more concerned with the size of their dicks than actually getting the job done.'

'Fair enough,' admitted Brenner. 'So, what now?'

'Hey, Ded, I can't spoon feed you, dude. I found the target, now you gotta pull the trigger. I advise getting your butt to Los Angeles ASAP. The delegates have all already arrived and I would guess time is of the freaking essence here. Things could go bad at any moment.'

'Thanks, Griff,' said Brenner. 'I owe you one.'

'Yeah. You do,' confirmed Griff. 'Just don't die, OK?'

'Copy that,' said Brenner as he hung up. Then he picked up the room phone and dialed Solomon's room. 'Got news,' he said. 'Come to mine.'

Less than sixty seconds later, both Howard and Solomon were there, and Brenner gave them the run down.

Solomon got straight on to his cell phone and barked a string of instructions.

'Right,' he said, as he rang off. 'We

have an X-copter arriving at the local airport in half an hour. Pack up and let's go. Brenner, you can leave your rat bike at the hotel or at the airport. I would recommend the airport, as that's where we're going to leave the BMW, and I would hazard a guess it will be more secure. You can come back and pick it up later. If you're still alive.'

'Airport it is then,' agreed the big man.

Less than an hour later they were aboard the X-copter and heading for Los Angeles at almost three hundred miles an hour.

CHAPTER 36

Why couldn't everyone be as efficient as the Germans? Wondered the chancellor to herself. After all, she had ordered room service over an hour ago. OK, to be fair, she had ordered off menu, but then again, what sort of civilized country didn't have *Fischbrötchen*? After all, it was simply a pickled fish sandwich. How could it be so difficult to obtain?

As she sat and waited, her blood sugar level dropping like an elevator with a snapped cable, her famous temper began to boil.

But just before she could throw one of her epic tantrums, the door burst open and her personal assistant rushed in.

'Ah,' exclaimed the chancellor. '*Meine Fischbrötchen.*'

The assistant shook her head. '*Nein, meine kanzler. Nein Fischbrötchen.* Please, madam chancellor. We are under attack. The building has been compromised and security advise that we should evacuate immediately.'

'And what about my *Fischbrötchen?*'

The assistant stared blankly for a full second before she reacted. 'Madam chancellor,' she shouted. 'With all due respect, fuck your stupid fish sandwich. People are dying. Now follow me so we can get the hell out of here.'

The security detail formed a hard diamond formation around the sandwichless chancellor and they headed for the fire escape.

***

Yuri loved America. More than he loved Russia. But that was easy, because he thought his mother country sucked ass. Freezing cold in winter, wet all July, and barely acceptable for the rest of the year.

Not like Los Angeles. Winters at sixty-eight degrees, summer at around seventy-five. Half the amount of rain. And to top it all, Hollywood. Who the hell wouldn't love a country that embodied the wealth and fame and glitz and glamor that was the film industry.

Yeah, America was a country where money talked, and bullshit walked. And Yuri and his friends had loads of money. Truckloads of the stuff. Because it is amazing how much wealth you can amass in a short time when you literally rape and plunder your own countries assets.

And the best part of the whole thing was, everyone in the president's party had diplomatic immunity. It was fantastic, you could commit any misdemeanor you wanted and get out of it by simply flashing your passport and saying the magic words, diplomatic immunity.

Although, to be honest, Yuri wasn't exactly sure what his official designation was. He was carrying a weapon. A soviet issue P-96 with two extra magazines. So maybe he was part of the security team. Or maybe he had simply been issued a weapon and he was part of the advisory board.

He scratched his head and thought for a while. He seemed to remember someone mentioning entertainments officer. Or something similar. It was difficult to put his finger on it as he had been horrendously drunk at the time his cousin had offered him the position. Oh well, he was sure he would find out sooner rather than later. Now was the time for partying.

Speaking of which, Yuri could hear a crowd of his compatriots shouting and dancing in the corridor. He picked up one of the bottles of Cristal champagne he had ordered and opened the door to his room.

To be greeted by utter chaos.

The noise he had taken for partying was actually the sound of utter panic. People were running up and down the corridor like ants in a fire. No rhyme nor reason to their apparent movement. Some were shouting orders, others were countermanding those orders and yet others were simply shouting.

Yuri grabbed one of the women as she ran past and pulled her close. 'What the hell is going on?' he asked.

She shook her head frantically. 'I'm not sure,' she blurted. 'But I think we are under attack. Terrorists of some sort. There are bodies everywhere. Let me go.'

'Why?' shouted Yuri. 'Where are you going to?'

The woman hesitated for a moment then burst into tears. 'I don't know,' she admitted. 'Are you security?' she asked.

'Yes,' said Yuri. 'I think so. Actually, I'm not sure. I have a gun,' he continued, drawing his P-96.

'Good enough,' stated the woman. 'Everyone,' she shouted out. 'I've found one of the security guards. Gather round.'

And the chaos started to slowly congeal into some form of order, as everyone gathered around Yuri, waiting for him to lead them.

Yuri stared at his new-found flock and rolled his eyes.

'Fuck,' he murmured to himself. 'And everything was going so well.'

CHAPTER 37

The German security team split into four sections. Four of the twelve formed a hard diamond around the chancellor, three took up the rear, three more formed an arrowhead formation in front of her and the final two ranged ahead as an advance team, checking and clearing before allowing the chancellor to move from room to room. All had their weapons drawn. Either a Heckler and Koch P30 pistol or a Heckler and Koch MP5 sub machine gun. They also all wore audio links, attached to their collars with throat mikes and in-ear phones.

At the moment they were in the stairwell leading to the corridor on the third floor of the luxury apartment building the German government had rented. The two forward reconnaissance men opened the door into the corridor and did a quick scan.

'Wait,' instructed the leader into his

throat mike as they walked down the corridor, stopping at each door, opening it, and checking the room. 'Clear,' he announced as they checked the last room. 'Bring the chancellor in.'

The arrowhead came in first, followed by the hard diamond. And even though the men on point had already checked each room, the three men in the arrow formation rechecked, leaving nothing to chance.

The tail followed, walking slowly backwards, covering the rear.

'Proceeding to next floor,' announced the leader.

But as they headed for the door to the fire escape, it opened. And through it walked a man in a deep-cowl hooded top. He appeared to be crippled. A badly hunched back and malformed legs. Or maybe no legs at all, maybe blades that curved backwards. Behind him, another man. This one seemed normal apart from his hideously humped back.

'Halt,' commanded the team leader as he drew a bead on the cripple.

But the newcomer kept walking forward, moving with an odd jerky gait, his head held low, so it was impossible to see his face.

'Halt now,' shouted the leader. 'Or I will be forced to use lethal force. This is your last warning.'

The odd man continued to advance, as did the man behind him. Not reacting at all, not showing any aggression, but neither showing any sign of stopping.

The leader glanced at his companion. 'Maybe they're deaf,' he ventured.

The companion shrugged. 'Two deaf cripples. Could be, but not likely. Try a warning shot.'

The leader nodded, lined up his pistol and fired. The slug whistled past the advancing man's ear and struck the wall behind him.

No visible reaction. Not even the slightest flinch.

The team leader fired again. This time the bullet struck the floor directly in front of the foremost intruder.

This time he stopped and looked up, pulling back his hood as he did so. A long canine-like snout, massive teeth, burning, bloodshot yellow eyes.

'*Was zur Hölle?*' grunted the leader. 'What the hell is that thing?'

'Shoot it,' yelled his companion.

Without any further hesitation, both of them opened up on the abomination standing in front of them. One with his P30 and the other with his MP5. Thirty rounds tore into the thing in front of them, but it did nothing to slow it down. It kept moving forward with the same, implacable jerking gate.

Then it pulled back its lips and howled. A laughing, shuddering wail that set one's teeth on edge and made one's hair stand up in deep primal fear.

'Retreat,' shouted the leader. 'Get the chancellor out of here. Barricade the doors as you go. Hans and I will stay here and slow it down. Move, move.'

The security detail moved like the well-oiled machine that they were, reversing their movement and retreating. Slamming the door behind them and ramming a rubber wedge into it to jam it closed.

In the corridor, the leader and Hans changed magazines and opened fire once again.

It had the same effect as shooting at a sheet of armor plate.

Then the thing was on them. Teeth

tearing and claws raking. Blood sprayed high, painting the corridor, and flooding the carpet.

Behind the permanent, Osiris grinned at seeing the carnage, his large canines reflecting the overhead lighting, his bloodshot eyes crinkled in pleasure.

And the permanent moved forward again, smashing down the door with consummate ease.

It walked into a hail of gunfire as three more of the security team, opened fire at almost point-blank range. Full metal jacket slugs buzzed and whined as they ricocheted about the corridor like a swarm of hornets. The things clothes were shredded by the massive amounts of lead being thrown at it, but its forward momentum didn't slacken by one iota.

Three more brave men died. Torn limb from limb. But this time, the *Hyaenidae* hesitated. Stopping as the heady aroma of blood filled its olfactory organs, and the delicious salty flavor of human blood and offal piqued its hunger.

With a grunt of pleasure, it settled down on its haunches and started to feed, ripping open the gut cavities of the fallen and feasting on their livers and kidneys, snuffling, and whining as it did so.

Osiris morphed into hyena mode and joined in, his animal instincts driving out his human logic as their target made good their escape.

The German security detail headed for the roof, calling for assistance as they did so, hoping for a helicopter evacuation.

CHAPTER 38

Two of the British security team were already down. They had attempted to stop two suspicious looking men entering the building. One was dressed in a hooded track suit top that covered his face entirely. He also had an outrageously large hump on his back.

The other, although dressed normally, had a matching hump. The security team were both concerned that the men might be concealing something in some sort of a back pack. Most likely a suicide bomb of some sort.

They had stood in front of the suspects and demanded that they stop and allow themselves to be searched. However, without even breaking stride, the lead man simply ripped their heads off and cast them aside like discarded candy wrappers.

Needless to say, everyone else in the vicinity had gone insane, albeit in a typically British way.

Shouts of, *goodness me*, and, *that's not right*, echoed through the hallways as staff ran for cover. Meanwhile, upstairs, the rest of the team had barricaded themselves in the prime minister's room with guards both inside and outside.

They had also radioed for help, and both SWAT and the Secret Service were rushing to their aid.

The head of the security B-team had just boiled the kettle and furnished the prime minister with a cup of tea. She sat at the table, facing the barricaded door. Her hand shook slightly as she took a sip.

'Help should be arriving shortly, ma'am,' informed her B-team leader.

'Exactly what sort of threat are we facing?' asked the PM.

The B-team leader, Hugo Bonneville, shook his head. 'To be honest, ma'am, not that sure. The last communication that we heard from Perkins, just before he went down, was the word, *hyena*. I've got your assistant online in an attempt to see if that collates with any known terrorist group at large at the moment. Frankly though, it doesn't ring a bell. Not the sort of nomenclature that the average terrorist group would assign themselves, hyenas being a less than salubrious beast, as it were. Normally they go for eagles, or lions or such what. You know the type, the lions of Islam, or the eagles of freedom. Perhaps even scorpions. But vultures or hyenas, not to my knowledge. No one wants to be in a movement known as the Vultures of Allah, or the Hyenas of truth. Doesn't make sense.'

Outside the PM's suite, the eight-man A-team had stripped the adjacent rooms of all furniture and used it to block the corridor, wedging beds, chairs, and tables together so tightly that it would take a wrecking ball to dislodge them.

Or a *Hyaenidae*.

Set struck the door first, buckling its hinges and popping the handle. But the linked maze of furniture held it closed.

'Hold,' called out the British A-team leader, his voice low and controlled. 'Fire only on my command.'

The next time, both Set and the permanent ran into the door together. The entire corridor shook with the power of the blow but still the latticework held, keeping the door firmly shut.

Again, and again the two *Hyaenidae* slammed against the obstacle, and slowly the pieces of furniture began to splinter and break.

'Bloody hell, sir,' gasped one of the men. 'What on earth could that be?'

'Steady, Rickmansworth,' commanded the A-team leader. 'Calm down, I'm sure we shall see what it is soon enough.'

There was a pause and, with a final gargantuan effort, the two *Hyaenidae* burst through.

'Well, bugger me,' stated the A-team leader laconically. 'Now there's something a chap doesn't see every day. On my mark, three, two, one, fire.'

The eight-man team opened fire.

'Aim for the eyes, gentlemen,' advised the leader. 'The rest of them seems jolly well bulletproof.'

The team adjusted their aim, concentrating their gunfire on the hyena men's eyes.

But alas, their eyes were just as bullet resistant as the rest of their bodies and, although the combined accurate firepower did slow them down a jot, they were amongst the team in under ten seconds.

The A-team leader thumbed his throat mike. 'Bonneville, old chap,' he communicated to the B-team inside the PMs suite. 'Afraid we've been bested. Two assailants. Seem to be some sort of biological bastard cross between a man and a hyena. God save the Queen and all that. Simmonds out and good luck.'

He burned off the last of his magazine, then, at the last moment, pulled out a L109A1 fragmentation grenade, pulled the pin, jumped onto Set's back, and held it against the *Hyaenidae's* head.

'Take that, you hellhound,' he yelled.

The resultant explosion ripped Simmonds apart, but unfortunately, although it did knock Set off his feet, it did little else to damage the hyena man.

Inside the suite the B-team braced for impact.

Bonneville, the team leader, flipped over the table the PM was sitting at and placed it in front of her. 'Don't worry, ma'am,' he said. 'The chaps will ensure your safety. On the plus side, at least we know why Perkins blurted out the word, hyena before he kicked the bucket. Must say, that little conundrum was rather bothering me.'

'Jesus, Bonneville,' shrieked the prime minister. 'We're all going to fucking die.'

Bonneville sniffed his disapproval at the PM's outburst. 'Come along now, ma'am,' he said, his voice pitched low so as not to carry. 'It just won't do letting the chaps see you acting this way. Hold hard, we shall persevere.'

'No, we fucking won't,' snapped the prime minister. 'Those things, whatever they are, have killed everything that stood in their way, and we are no different.' The PM burst into tears. 'Oh, shit, I don't want to die. Not like this.'

Bonneville took a deep breath to control his temper. After all, he and his men were laying down their lives for this stupid bitch. And to think, he didn't even vote for her. 'Whatever, ma'am,' he said. 'Just try to keep a hold on yourself.'

The door shuddered as the *Hyaenidae* threw themselves at it and cracks started to appear on the wall. It wouldn't be long now. Less than a minute.

At that moment the window exploded, and a man dressed in an expensive suit and tie came crashing through, rolling on the floor before he stood to address the team leader.

'Captain Bonneville?'

Bonneville nodded.

'Commander Davidson. MI6. I've got a rope attached to one of the upper floors. Give me a hand to secure it to the PM and I can abseil her to the ground floor, we've got an armored vehicle standing by.'

'Righty-ho, commander,' replied Bonneville.

The two men grabbed the startled PM, clipped a rope around her waist and dragged her to the window just as the door burst open.

Commander Davidson threw Bonneville a quick salute. 'Well done, Captain,' he said. 'Cover our withdrawal, there's a good fellow.'

'God speed,' replied Bonneville. Then he turned and added his firepower to the rest of the team as they opened fire on the two hyena men.

By the time the *Hyaenidae* had killed everyone in the room, the PM was ensconced in a private armored vehicle and was leaving the scene at almost one hundred miles an hour, covered by two more armed vehicles and a Blackhawk helicopter.

Bonneville's last coherent thought before he died was one of satisfaction at a job well done.

CHAPTER 39

The X3 helicopter Solomon had ordered got them to Los Angles in just under two hours. And now they were hovering above the convention center.

The copilot was scanning all radio traffic and keeping them up to date with the current situation.

'Sounds like the British prime minister is in the clear,' he informed them. 'The Germans are calling for an assist. Apparently, they are on the roof of their apartment.'

The pilot spun the copter in a slow circle while they all looked for a group of people on top of one of the apartment blocks.

Shadow spotted them first, pulling on Brenner's sleeve and pointing.

'Over there,' said the big man.

The pilot banked hard right and headed for the building at top speed. 'We can only take one more passenger,'' he yelled.

'Maybe two, but this bird is built for speed, not payload.'

'Just get us in as close and as quickly as possible,' replied Brenner.

They were mere moments away from the building when they saw the door to the roof explode out, and two dog boys ran onto the rooftop. A leader and a permanent.

'Shit,' yelled Brenner. 'Times out, move it.'

The pilot rammed his yoke forward and went into a suicidal dive, pulling up less than ten feet from the roof. As he lowered the copter another few feet above the chancellor, Brenner leaned out, grabbed her by her arm and yanked her into the helicopter. He pulled so hard he actually felt her shoulder dislocate. But he felt a few breaks were far preferable to becoming *Hyaenidae* chow.

The pilot pulled up sharply, just before one of the dog boys grabbed at one of the skids in an attempt to yank the copter from the sky.

There was nothing they could do to stop the ensuing massacre.

The German security detachment died

bravely, but badly, as they were torn to shreds by the evil spawn of the colonel and the Bloodborn Project.

Brenner watched as the two *Hyaenidae* finished off their prey then bolted from the building.

'The Russians have incoming,' shouted the copilot. 'They're in the Ritz Hotel.' He pointed. 'President is in the penthouse suite. According to radio chatter, a bunch of those things are headed his way. They've already broken through the perimeter. It's a matter of minutes. Maybe less.'

'Drop us off on the roof,' said Brenner. 'Then take the chancellor to safety.

Solomon draped a thick woolen blanket over his head, covering up completely against the sun. 'Let's make this snappy,' he said. 'Once I'm inside, the sun won't be a problem. I hope.'

Brenner nodded, then he turned to the chancellor. 'We're going in, chancellor,' he said. 'But as soon as the pilot has dropped us off, they will take you to a safe area. It's all over. Nothing more to worry about.'

The chancellor nodded, her face as pale

as a shroud, her pupils dilated in serious shock, her breathing fast and ragged.

She looked at Brenner and said. *'Fischbrötchen.'*

The big man had no idea what the German politician was saying, so he simply gave her a thumbs up and nodded.

The copter flared up against the roof of the hotel and Brenner, Howard, Solomon, and Shadow piled out.

Seconds later it was gone, and they were alone on the roof, heading for the door that gained access to the building below.

The only person who carried a weapon was Howard. A Boys rifle. And the only reason he was carrying it was because Brenner had made him and Solomon promise they would take him out if he lost control of his inner wolf.

Because it was time to change.

He had no other option left to him.

CHAPTER 40

Yuri held up both his hands and called for silence. 'Quiet,' he shouted at the crowd of over twenty people who had gathered around him. 'Now, who amongst you has a weapon?'

One woman and six men held their hands up.

'So, I take it that you are official security?' he asked them.

There was a general mumble of conversation and eventually the woman answered. 'I think so. My cousin, Boris, didn't really say when he hired me. But surely you would know. Aren't you Yuri Popov?'

'Yes,' admitted Yuri. 'Why?'

'I was told that you were head of staff security.'

Yuri shook his head. 'No ways. If that were true, then surely I would know.'

There was a murmur of agreement amongst everyone. It was true, they agreed, he should know if he was head of security.

Yuri rubbed his temples with the heels of his hands. He was getting a headache. A real bad one. And worse than that, now he thought about it, he did seem to recall Boris saying something about running staff security. And when he had told him he knew nothing about it, Boris had assured him there was nothing to worry about. The president had his own core of professional guards, and Yuri would only be responsible for staff security, not presidential.

Shit, he exclaimed to himself. If only he hadn't been so drunk at the time. Curse Boris and his vodka.

'OK,' he shouted. 'All of you who aren't security, stick together and leave the building. I recommend you use the fire escape and not the elevators. The rest of you, the ones with weapons, follow me. We're going to protect our president.'

'I don't want to leave you guys,' answered one of the men without a weapon. 'You've got guns. All I've got is a pen and a new pair of Aviator sunglasses.'

'Well then put them on,' said Yuri. 'Then at least you look cool when the western media put you on television as you leave the building safely.'

The weaponless people started discussing the pros and cons of staying or leaving until Yuri blew a blood vessel.

'It is not a discussion,' he shouted. 'It is an order from the head of staff security. Form an orderly line and get the hell out of the building.' To emphasize his order, he pulled his pistol out and shot into the air. He immediately regretted it as his ears rang and he saw spots on front of his eyes from the muzzle flash

'Fuck,' he murmured to himself. 'I had no idea these things were so loud.'

Fortunately, his cavalier attitude towards gun safety did the trick and the non-security members formed a line and marched down the stairs.

Yuri did a quick head count and noticed he now only had five men and one woman. 'Hey,' he exclaimed. 'Where did the sixth man go?'

'That's Vadim,' said the woman. 'He is pussy. Rather he left. Is better.' She held her hand out. 'My name is Svetlana.'

Yuri took her hand. 'Greetings, Svetlana. By the order of the head of security, which appears to be me, I hereby make you second in charge. Well done on your promotion. Now let's go.'

Yuri led the way to the stairs and headed up towards the penthouse suite.

They only had two floors to climb so it didn't take them long. When they got to the penthouse, Yuri pushed at the door and was amazed to find it wasn't locked. He opened it to find a single guard. The guard nodded a greeting and Yuri strained his memory.

'Vassily Sokolov?' he greeted the man hesitantly.

'Yes. And you are Yuri Popov, the new head of staff security.'

Yuri nodded his agreement. 'Apparently. Look, Vassily, the building is under attack, why haven't you secured the door and the corridor?'

Vassily shrugged his head. 'The president ordered us not to. He is inside, waiting for the attackers. He said when they arrive he is going to teach them a lesson.'

Yuri let out a sigh of disbelief. 'What?

Is he mad?'

Vassily nodded. 'Totally. But he's also a real hard ass, so I am sure, when these terrorists arrive, he will show them a thing or to. After all, he is black belt in everything, apparently. And if it's a little beyond him, well, there are eight of us and we are all ex-Spetsnaz, so I have no doubt we can sort the problem out.'

The man's supreme level of confidence impressed Yuri and, for the first time in a while he felt at ease. 'So,' he said to Vassily. 'Can I take my group inside? Will the president mind?'

'Not at all,' answered Vassily. 'The bigger the audience, the better for him. Just knock and enter.'

Yuri did just that. He knocked, then filed into the penthouse, his motley crew of security behind him. Standing in the room were seven of the hardest looking men Yuri had ever seen. All around six feet. One hundred and eighty pounds. Not in suits like western style Secret Service agents, but instead in full battle kit. Ceramic plate body armor, Vityaz submachine guns, RGN fragmentation grenades and a shithouse full of attitude.

Standing in front of a dining room table, behind his security guards, was the president himself. Dressed in an expensive hand tailored British suit. Polished brogues, his wispy hair in a vague comb over. Sixty-five years old but looked sixty-two and acted twenty-three. Maybe five feet six inches, or five eleven if you believed the government owned daily newspaper, *Komsomolskaya Pravda.*

Yuri bowed deeply, as did the line of security guards behind him. '*Moy prezident, prostite moye vtorzheniye,*' he said. 'We were told we could enter.'

The president nodded and waved Yuri and his group to the side of the room. 'Welcome,' he said. 'Now wait and watch as your president shows these bastard terrorists a thing or two.'

Yuri nodded fervently and clutched his pistol like a talisman.

It didn't take long, and they heard the door that led to the corridor smash open. There was a brief shout from Vassily, then a sickening wet tearing sound.

And then silence.

Everyone waited with bated breath. Apart from the president, who was busy removing his suit jacket and rolling up his sleeves in readiness for his upcoming combat.

Then the door to the penthouse blasted into the room.

Three creatures walked in. One was ostensibly a man, apart from his massively hunched back, like he had a rucksack under his coat. But the two things behind him were denizens from the darkest pits of hell. Hyena-like faces, complete with slobbering jaws, huge teeth, and lolling tongues. Their maws were covered in blood, as was their tattered attire. Their yellow bloodshot eyes rolled in their heads like they were about to suffer an epileptic fit. And they walked with an odd stop-start movement, almost as if they were falling forward every time they took a step, their backwards bent legs jerking spasmodically as the moved forward.

The president's personal guard raised their weapons and were about to fire when the president held up his hand to stop them.

'Wait,' he commanded. 'I would like to talk first.'

Everyone in the room stopped what they

were doing. Even the *Hyaenidae*.

'Speak,' said Anubis, his voice a rasping growl.

'What are you?' asked the president.

'I am the new order,' answered Anubis.

'No,' denied the president. 'You are a mere animal. I am the most powerful leader in the world, I control armies, navies, an air force. I control the will of over one hundred and forty million Russians who would die for me if I so commanded. And now, it is time for you to leave.'

The president stepped forward and, with great speed, performed a flawless *mawashi geri*, or roundhouse kick. It was timed perfectly, arcing up towards Anubis' face, ready to land with enough force to smash a two-inch plank of oak.

But to the *Hyaenidae* it was as if the president was moving in ultra-slow motion. He watched the foot approach and, as it did, he morphed into his Hyena-man mode, still standing on his two legs but growing a foot in height, adding two hundred pounds to his mass, and extending his jaw and teeth.

As the president's foot came within

range, Anubis simply closed his jaw on the limb, severing the leg just above the knee with one bite.

The president fell to the floor with a scream of agony as blood pumped from his shattered arteries like a fire hose.

Then the two permanents fell on the president and tore him to shreds, growling and laughing and swallowing chunks of flesh as fast as they could.

The bodyguards opened fire and Anubis calmly set about smashing them into hamburger as the bullets buzzed and whined off his impenetrable skin.

Yuri and his security team cowered in the corner of the room as they watched the best of Russian military might get wiped out in mere seconds.

Then all the *Hyaenidae's* attention was on the hapless staff security team.

But before they could attack them, there was a sound from the corridor unlike anything Yuri had ever heard before. It rattled the windows and doors, vibrating the air at such amplitude the Russian could feel his insides move in sympathy.

It was the roar of an Alpha. Primal and atavistic, and it reached back into mankind's past and awoke every fear he had ever experienced. Every warning, every moment of dread and dismay.

It was the sound of death incarnate, and it was pissed.

Yuri looked up to see a seven-foot, four-hundred-pound Wolfman enter the room. Muscles like slabs of raw concrete, teeth the size of bayonets and claws that made Wolverine look like a child's nanny.

The monster grabbed one of the permanents and hammered it against the wall with such force that it smashed right through into one of the bedrooms, scattering bricks and rubble like shrapnel as it did.

And behind the monster came a man dressed all in black, and he moved like a wraith amongst shadows. Faster than it seemed possible, like bad stop motion photography, he flickered from one part of the room to the next, slashing and biting at the *Hyaenidae* as he did so.

'I've had enough of this shit,' yelled Yuri to no one in particular as he dashed for the door. 'Come on,' he yelled at his team. 'Let's get the fuck out of here.'

They followed Yuri out of the room, all

moving as fast as they could. Outside, in the corridor, Yuri saw a man holding the biggest rifle he had ever seen, and a girl who growled at them as they ran past.

But Yuri and his team didn't stop running until they had reached the ground floor and exited the building.

The last thing he noticed was that, as they exited, another four of the hyena monsters ran past them into the building and headed upstairs.

Yuri sprinted across the road and eventually stopped behind an armored vehicle, falling to the floor, and throwing up as he did so.

Finally, he rolled over on his back and stared up at the blue sky above, his chest heaving as he tried to calm his breathing.

'Fuck this country,' he said to himself. 'I'm never going to leave Russia again, I don't care how cold it gets.'

CHAPTER 41

Brennerwolf picked up one of the permanents, held it above his head, and smacked it down on his knee, breaking it's back as he did so. Tossing the limp body aside he turned to face Anubis, slashing and kicking as fast as he could. The Alpha *Hyaenidae* fought back, biting and grappling. Brenner was faster and, as a trained combat expert, a superior warrior. But the hyena-man hybrid was stronger. And Brenner could see that one bite from those massive jaws would result in a life-threatening injury. Even for the Wolfman. So, he worked at a distance, fighting like a boxer, jabbing, and hooking.

But as he did so, the permanent who he had just dispatched, healed, and leapt onto Brenner's back, snapping at his neck. Brenner dropped and rolled to dislodge the creature, reaching behind him to grab it and throw it across the room.

Solomon was using his superior speed

to engage, dashing in and out in lightning quick bursts. Slashing, biting, and retreating, leaving the *Hyaenidae* with deep, bleeding wounds. But, no matter how deep they were, the cuts healed within seconds, hindering the dog boys but doing little else.

Howard was doing his best to help, using the massive power of his Boys anti-tank rifle in an effort to slow the hyena men down. But, like Brenner's efforts, the results were temporary, knocking them down, sometimes even causing them injury, but only for seconds at a time.

After five minutes of unbelievably intense combat it became apparent Doctor Mengele and the Bloodborn Project had created a weapon capable of defeating the Wolfman. The power of a tactical nuclear missile controlled by a mind not seen since the likes of Genghis Khan, or Hitler.

A perfect storm of insanity, megalomania, and unstoppable strength.

Anubis had told the Russian prime minister that he was the new order. And he had been correct.

Nothing short of a thermobaric bomb could stop him.

With a howl of rage, Set and two permanents managed to grab Solomon and hammer him into the wall repeatedly until he slid to the floor. Conscious but limp, as almost every bone in his body was broken. The formula that raged inside him battled to heal the fractures, but he was exhausted beyond belief and, although he might live, he would not be moving for a while.

Howard had taken cover behind some scattered furniture in the corridor, pulling Shadow down next to him, fully aware that his rifle was doing little more than irritate the hyena men.

And Brennerwolf stood alone, back against the wall, a wolf at bay. Around him, arrayed in a semicircle, five slobbering, wild eyed abominations of nature. Blood ran down Brennerwolf's body as his recuperative powers struggled to heal the myriad of cuts and tears in his flesh. His left arm hung loosely by his side, broken in at least three places, and his chest heaved as he forced oxygen into his lungs, ignoring the pain of his shattered ribs.

'What are you?' growled Anubis.

'I am retribution,' replied Brennerwolf.

The hyena men laughed, their amusement an insane cackle.

'Whatever you are,' continued Anubis. 'You are broken.'

'Yes,' agreed Brennerwolf. 'It appears I am.'

'And now you die,' stated the Alpha *Hyaenidae*.

Brennerwolf didn't reply. He had nothing to say. Outgunned at every level, he stood tall and prepared himself for the final onslaught.

And the hyena boys didn't disappoint. At first, they all attacked at once, punching, clawing, and biting. Ripping chunks of flesh from the Wolfman, breaking bones, and tearing muscle. But when Brennerwolf finally fell to his knees, they stopped and stood back.

Then, with terrifying mundanity, they lined up and took turns beating him. One punch or kick then they would revolve to the back of the queue. A production line of torture.

First, they broke his jaw. Then his ribs, one by one. His right arm. His left leg. His wrist. His orbital socket. The ragged ends of bone stuck out through his ruptured flesh, like broken tombstones in a blood-soaked cemetery.

But still he would not fall to the floor, remaining on his knees, grunting with the pain and effort it took to stop from passing out. Willing himself to stay upright. To refuse the final insult.

He heard a scream and saw Shadow running towards him, flailing at the hyena boys as she came. Desperately trying to defend him. But he raised his ruined arm and sent her back. No need for her to die as well.

He strained his eyes, but he could no longer see. The world had degenerated into a wash of black and white shapes. Indistinct. Incomprehensible.

He couldn't even hear the sounds of the blows landing on him anymore. His mind and body, numb.

Then, far away, he heard a children's choir. Their voices high and sweet. The unsullied sound of innocence. And someone spoke. But he couldn't hear the words.

Slowly the world began to tilt. He was going to fall, and he no longer had the strength to stop himself.

But the voice persisted. Becoming strident. Cutting through the mist of his pain and befuddlement.

Brennerwolf smiled. It was Mister Bolin. Cantankerous old fucker. Couldn't he see Brennerwolf was dying?

'You need to change. Unless you do, then all is lost. You are the only one who can go up against these hyena abominations and win. But only if you change. Only if you assume your true form.'

And Brennerwolf laughed out loud, blood spraying from his broken jaws. For there was no Mister Bolin. He was simply remembering the last conversation they had together.

And anyway, their advice had been for naught, he had changed. He had given all. And he had been found wanting.

'Assume your true form,' the voice urged. *'Unless you do, then all is lost.'*

'Go away,' mumbled Brennerwolf through his shattered teeth.

He heard another scream. He looked up and his vison cleared just enough to see that Anubis had grabbed Shadow by her neck and was slapping her repeatedly, a savage grin on his face as her skin split and her blood flew.

'No,' said Brennerwolf as he dragged himself back onto one knee.

'No,' he repeated. And all around him it seemed as though he was wreathed in the deepest shadow. A cloak of darkness.

'No!' he shouted at the top of his voice.

The flesh on his back split open to revel the shining white bones of his ribs. Then each rib split and sprang from his back like a ghoulish hand, bones flayed outwards. Then they started to grow, rippling skyward, white vines, twisting, and reforming and spreading. Between each rib grew a skein of muscle. And the muscle grew a covering of black feathers, each one as large as a grown man's forearm.

Brennerwolf stood up. And as he did so, his wounds knitted back together, bones reforming, flesh and muscle becoming whole once more.

Then, with the sound akin to a tsunami booming against the shoreline, he opened his newly formed wings. They spanned the room, thirty feet wide, shimmering with a blue white fire and vibrating with untold power.

And all before him was as naught. Paltry and insignificant. For he was no longer Brennerwolf.

He was the sword of Samael. The venom of the Lord and the right hand of Death. He was Hemah.

He was Wrath.

And he grasped Set and destroyed him, tearing him in half with one twist of his mighty arms. Then did he dispose of Osiris and his bastard siblings, the permanents. Blood did flow freely as their lives were extinguished and their souls liberated.

Finally, he did face Anubis, the Alpha. He commanded the *Hyaenidae* release the human girl. This the abomination did, sinking to his knees and groveling.

But still, he died screaming, as Wrath shows no mercy.

Then Hemah looked upon the others in the room. He saw their sin and was not pleased, knowing they should suffer for it.

'Brenner,' shouted Shadow.

The being that was once Brenner stared at the human, and he saw her flaws, her shortcomings. Her essential humanity.

'Brenner,' she shouted again, as she ran to him, throwing her arms around him and holding him tight. 'It's over,' she said as she looked up at him, her eyes full of love. 'Come back to us.'

Wrath hesitated. And the wings of darkness shrunk back and withered.

And Brenner said. 'Shadow, you can talk.'

CHAPTER 42

Howard called the X-copter to evacuate them from the roof of the Ritz hotel before they were apprehended by security.

Brenner carried Solomon, cradling him to his chest like a babe, wincing at the sound of his broken bones grating together.

No one spoke on the two-hour trip back to the airport in St. George, Utah. Solomon lay still, his body healing. Howard was as taciturn as usual, and Shadow simply held Brenner's hand and stared at him, her eyes full of concern.

But Brenner seemed to be in a state of shock. He had only vague recollections of what had happened to him. The change. Wolfman to … he wasn't sure. Memories of power filled his mind. Tearing apart the *Hyaenidae* with utmost ease.

Alien thoughts. Non-human, superior and unforgiving. Feelings as sharp and jagged as crystal. Flawless. Black and white.

As opposed to the usual mélange of shade that governed the human thought process.

Wings stretching out to infinity, as black as the abyss. Knowledge, all encompassing, severe and merciless.

And then Shadow's voice, bringing him back from the void. Reminding him of his humanity, before he had unleashed a terrible power on the world. Before he had punished all for their sins.

Before he had let slip the horsemen of the apocalypse.

And what little he did remember terrified him absolutely.

Who was he?

What was he?

He thought back on what Mister Bolin had said. *'You need to change. Unless you do, then all is lost. You are the only one who can go up against these hyena abominations and win. But only if you change. Only if you assume your true form.'*

Was that his true form. That pitiless warrior. That paragon of virtue.

That ... thing?

Solomon broke Brenner's train of

thought as he groaned and opened his eyes. 'Wow,' he exclaimed. 'Those dog boys worked me over properly.' He looked at Brenner. 'But you sorted them out. Knew you had it in you.'

'You saw what I became?' asked Brenner.

Solomon nodded.

'And that doesn't scare you?'

This time the man in black shrugged. 'Yes. No. You seemed to be on our side.'

'Yeah,' said Brenner. 'Seemed to be. It wasn't me, though. It was like some other being had taken over. Something completely unfamiliar. Inhuman. And I mean that, not a single trace of humanity. And if that doesn't scare you, then it should. It fucking terrifies me.'

'You think too much,' said Solomon. 'It's you. Just another mode. Like, super winged Wolfman. Or something. Not sure. Whatever, it kicks ass. The colonel said you could do it.'

'Yeah,' agreed Brenner. 'Which brings up the next step.'

Solomon nodded. 'Payback,' he said. 'I know. Tell you what, let's put off any planning until we've all had a bit of R&R.

I think my legs are still broken. We get back to the hotel. Sleep for a few days. Eat everything we can lay our hands on. Then plan our retribution. Agreed?'

Agreed,' confirmed Brenner.

CHAPTER 43

As per agreement, they did nothing for almost two days. Once again, Brenner shared a room with Shadow but, like before, she didn't talk, relying on gestures and expressions instead. But the big man didn't allow it to frustrate him. She would talk when she wanted to talk. *Hell,* he thought to himself. *I'm not even sure I heard her talk anyway, so no biggie.*

At the end of the second day, Solomon knocked on his door and walked in, Howard trailing behind him.

Sitting down he faced Brenner. 'I've been thinking,' he said. 'We both agree the colonel has gone too far.'

Brenner nodded but remained silent. He knew this wasn't easy for Solomon. After all, the colonel and the Project had been Solomon's rock or over fifty years. His sole focus of belief. To him the Project still equated to America, justice, and equality. To even entertain the thoughts he was having must have felt tantamount to betrayal. Treason.

'And the only way to stop him is to …'

The man in black hesitated. Unable to bring himself to voice the obvious conclusion to what he was saying.

'He has to be taken out,' said Brenner, his voice low and even. Attempting to be as gentle as possible.

Solomon sighed. 'Yes, 'he agreed. 'That. But, and now stay with me here, there's no reason for you to get involved. For me, the act would be simple. I return to base, report to the colonel as required. And do it. Why put you at risk?'

Brenner nodded. 'True,' he admitted. 'That's one way to look at it. However, what then? There's no way you can hide the fact you took the colonel out. It's an open and shut case.'

Solomon laughed. But there was no mirth. 'True. But let them try to arrest me.'

'They wouldn't have to,' said Brenner. 'All they would have to do is find a way to keep you separated from the formula. Then how long would you have?'

Solomon shrugged. 'A week. Maybe more. Not sure.'

'So, it would be a suicide mission?' confirmed the big man.

'Everyone dies eventually,' said Solomon. 'Even you and I, Brenner. And at least I would have done some good before I go.'

'No,' said Brenner. 'I heard you out and, after careful contemplation I must tell you your plan sucks ass.'

Solomon laughed again. This time it was genuine. 'Careful contemplation? You gave it all of two seconds thought. At most. OK, what's your plan?'

'Simple, the same as always. I go in, I remove everyone that needs removing, I get out.'

'Good plan,' said Solomon. 'Perhaps we could refine it a little. Tell you what, if you're adamant you should do this, why don't we get a little subtler than you usually are? Here's what we'll do, I give you a full plan of the facility. Then, I set up a meeting with the colonel at his office. I'll spin him some bullshit yarn about something or other. I text you when I'm ready, you come in, dispatch them, kick the crap out of me so I don't look complicit, then leave. Problem solved.'

The big man held out his hand and Solomon took it.

Deal,' he said. 'We leave tomorrow.'

***

The next morning when Solomon came to Brenner's room he was surprised to find Shadow in tears, her eyes red rimmed from crying. Opposite her, Brenner stood with a stony expression on his face. On the bed, her small rucksack was packed.

'What gives?' asked the man in black.

'It's time Shadow went her own way,' answered Brenner, his voice betraying no emotion. 'I've given her enough money, she can get the Greyhound to some place civilized. Start a life.'

Solomon didn't say anything. If Brenner wanted to ostracize one of his few friends, then far be it for him to argue. He wasn't the big man's keeper and he was sure Brenner had his reasons.

Finally, Shadow picked up her rucksack, gave Brenner one last pleading look, and left the room.

The two men stood in silence for a while.

'Why?' asked Solomon.

'She was becoming reliant on me,' answered Brenner. 'And that's not a good thing. Her life span will be considerably increased by being any place I am not. It's for the best.'

Solomon looked closely at the big man and saw straight through his flinty façade. 'Mistake,' he said. 'She's really into you. And, trust me on this, feelings like that are hard to come by.'

'It's for the best,' repeated Brenner.

Solomon shook his head. 'Whatever. Let's get moving.'

CHAPTER 44

Two days later, Brenner waited outside the chain link fence surrounding the Project. The forest had been cut back a hundred feet from the fence to expose a killing ground, watched over by a series of guard towers.

Usually a military facility such as this would be lit up like a summer's day at noon, with massive floodlights. But the colonel had decided to go for subtle instead. Often the less attention a facility garnered, the less likely it was to get broken into. To the untrained eye, this looked more like a well-guarded corporate facility, as opposed to a government sponsored, highly illegal, gene-splicing experimentation laboratory.

Granted, the guards were most likely equipped with infrared and there would be motion detectors, old fashioned trip wires and probably dogs. But none of that bothered Brenner.

When he was in Wolfman mode he was virtually undetectable. Too fast for motion detectors, too subtle for visual acquisition and too careful to fall foul of tripwires or the like.

And as for dogs, the moment Brennerwolf came anywhere near one, they simply rolled over to expose their bellies and waited for permission to rise.

His cell phone buzzed, and he checked it out. A one-word text from Solomon. 'Go.'

So, he did, changing into Wolfman mode, and at the same time, inuring himself. Gathering his essential humanity close. Putting it to the fore. He was Brenner. He was Wolf. He was Brennerwolf and he would not harm the innocent. Ever.

Then he leapt over the twenty-foot fence in a single bound, landing and launching immediately into a sprint, dashing from shadow to shadow. Ethereal. Wraithlike.

Four hundred pounds of virtual invisibility.

Keeping track of where he was by referring to the map that he had loaned from Solomon, the Wolfman darted from building to building until he was on target. He tested the door leading into the colonel's building and, as Solomon had promised, it had been left unlocked, so he ghosted in. Down the corridor, first left, second right.

It was just like any other door. Unadorned by name, a simple room number in black stenciled numbers. 53a.

Brennerwolf turned the handle and walked in.

As he did so, he heard two things happen simultaneously.

Firstly, a series of steel shutters slammed down over the door and the single window opposite him and, secondly, the combined thump of at least three rifles firing together.

And, like magic, three massive hypodermic darts bristled from his chest, like the quills of a porcupine.

He looked up to see the colonel, Doctor Mengele, five armed guards and Solomon.

The guards who had shot him had already dropped their tranquilizer guns and swopped them out for the South African made Denel NTW-20. A rifle chambered for a 20mm anti-aircraft round. It was the big brother to the Boys rifle that Howard had been carrying and Brenner knew that even one of those rounds was capable of punching right through him at a range of a mile, let alone from just across the room.

'You set me up,' he said to Solomon.

The man in black nodded. 'I'm sorry, big man,' he replied. 'Really, I am. But you see, the Project needs you. Even more now that we've seen your full potential.

Brennerwolf took a deep breath in an attempt to combat the industrial strength tranquilizer that was pumping through his veins. 'But the things that the colonel did,' he said. 'The innocent deaths. The families.'

Solomon had the grace to look embarrassed. 'Yes,' he agreed. 'Terrible. But you see, only the colonel has the strength to do such a thing. Only he has the courage to make such a sacrifice.'

'You're all fucking insane,' said Brennerwolf. 'It doesn't take courage to order the deaths of civilians. Quite the opposite. I thought you were my friend.'

'I am,' said Solomon. 'That's why I am doing this. I'm doing it for you, so that you can help your country. Now just relax. Don't struggle, the tranquilizers will kick in soon. This is for the best. You have just seen the sort of enemies that we face.'

'Fuck you,' shouted Brennerwolf. 'They were your insane products that became the enemy. Without you they wouldn't even have existed. You can't create an enemy then use that to justify what you're doing. You're all fucking mental.'

The colonel smiled. 'Whatever, Sergeant Brenner. Game set and match to us.'

With a sneer on his face, Brennerwolf reached into a pocket on his webbing belt that was slung around his neck and pulled out two items.

With a shaking hand he flicked the plastic top off the one to expose a needle that he plunged into his own neck.

Antidote,' he said as he felt the drug go to work, counteracting the tranquilizers.

'And that,' Solomon asked, pointing at the small object in Brennerwolf's other hand.

Brenner pushed a button and the object emitted a small beep. 'Homing beacon,' he answered.

'For what?' asked Solomon.

'Guided missile.' He threw himself to the floor.

The wall disintegrated in a vast ball of flame. Masonry and steel and glass whipped and spun around the room, slamming into the occupants who were still standing upright and were exposed to the full fury of the blast.

The roof tore off, and the carpet and furniture started to burn, filling the room with smoke.

And by the time that the smoke had cleared, Brennerwolf had disappeared and Solomon was the only one standing. He peered through the thinning smoke to see that Doctor Mengele had been literally torn in half.

Another quick glance revealed the colonel's head, separated by a few feet from the colonel's body. Both injuries the work of the Wolfman, the vicious claw marks obvious proof.

The guards lay in various random positions, all dead.

In the background, alarm sirens whooped out their strident calls to arms, searchlights swung back and forth, and illumination flares filled the sky.

But Solomon didn't even bother moving. He knew that the Wolfman had long gone.

He smiled. 'Well played, my friend,' he said in a whisper. 'Well played.'

And beyond the fence, deep in the forest, Brenner morphed back into human mode and walked up to the Winnebago.

Griff and Shadow were still busy dismantling the tripod for the Spike high explosive missile that they had launched.

Shadow looked up first and, squealing with excitement, she ran up to the naked big man and threw her arms around him, holding him as tightly as she could.

'So, he double-crossed you,' said Griff.

'Yep,' replied Brenner. 'Although I don't think that's how he saw it.'

'They try to tranquilize you first?'

'Yep. But the antidote worked fine.'

'Knew it would,' said Griff.

They shook hands

'Thanks, Griff.'

The old man waved Brenner's comment away. 'No worries. Now, let's get the hell out of here,' he said. 'But first,' he added. 'Put some pants on. Bloody show off.'

EPILOGUE

Brenner stood next to the white Crown Vic and looked at his log cabin. It had taken Shadow and him six months to build. Two bedrooms, a bathroom, large open plan living area with a wraparound porch.

They had leased the land from Grandma Becket, and they were now neighbours. Sheriff Colson had retired and had used his package to purchase Busby's bar. He ran the place on a flexitime basis, opening more or less when he felt like it. Usually, Wednesdays and Fridays.

When he did have a hankering to open he would always call Shadow, who would drive on down and help out.

The townsfolk of Backlash had unanimously voted Brenner in as the new sheriff.

Brenner waved at Shadow, then he adjusted his badge, climbed into the Crown Vic, and headed for town. He didn't carry a pistol. There was no need.

And far away, the sound of a children's choir shimmered in the air. And two old men raised their shot glasses and watched.

And waited…